POPCORN DAYS AND BUTTERMILK NIGHTS

When Carley landed in Norsten, Minnesota he knew one thing: this place had nothing to offer him. He certainly didn't expect to learn anything from his poverty-stricken relatives. Their way of life seemed harsher than anything he's seen in Minneapolis. But nothing he'd seen prepared him for David. His uncle, working in his blacksmith shop, possessed skills and knowledge that Carley was only beginning to appreciate, and a manner that offered Carley hope. Hope that he could one day understand the rage that burned within him, that erupted in outbursts of violence he could not understand and could not control, that had made this trip to Norsten his last chance. Now as the grim fall days approached—the time of popcorn days and buttermilk nights—Carley began to feel David's magic working in him, as surely as the heat of the forge and the fall of the hammer worked their magic on hard steel.

PUFFIN BOOKS BY GARY PAULSEN

Hatchet   *(A Newbery Honor Book)*
Dogsong   *(A Newbery Honor Book)*
Sentries
Tracker
Dancing Carl
Popcorn Days and Buttermilk Nights

Available in 1990:

The Foxman
Tiltawhirl John

Popcorn Days
&
Buttermilk
Nights

Gary Paulsen

PUFFIN BOOKS

PUFFIN BOOKS

A division of Penguin Books USA Inc.
375 Hudson Street, New York, New York 10014
Penguin Books Ltd, 27 Wrights Lane, London W8 5TZ, England
Penguin Books Australia Ltd, Ringwood, Victoria, Australia
Penguin Books Canada Ltd, 10 Alcorn Avenue, Toronto, Ontario, Canada M4V 3B2
Penguin Books (N.Z.) Ltd, 182–190 Wairau Road, Auckland 10, New Zealand

Penguin Books Ltd, Registered Offices: Harmondsworth, Middlesex, England

First published in the United States of America by E.P. Dutton,
a division of Penguin Books USA Inc., 1983
Published in Puffin Books, 1989
9 10 8
Copyright © Gary Paulsen, 1983
All rights reserved

No character in this book is intended to represent any actual person;
all the incidents of the story are entirely fictional in nature.

LIBRARY OF CONGRESS CATALOGING-IN-PUBLICATION DATA
Paulsen, Gary.
Popcorn days & buttermilk nights / Gary Paulsen.   p.   cm.
Reprint. Originally published: New York : Dutton, c1983.
Summary: Carley recalls the extraordinary summer when, as a
troubled fourteen-year-old, he first came to northern Minnesota to
stay with his blacksmith Uncle David and gained not only new skills
but also a new sense of himself.
ISBN 0-14-034204-4
[1. Uncles—Fiction.   2. Blacksmiths—Fiction.   3. Farm life—
Fiction.   4. Minnesota—Fiction.]   I. Title.   II. Title: Popcorn
days and buttermilk nights.
[PZ7.P2843Po 1989]   [Fic]—dc20   89-33408

Printed in the United States of America
Set in Janson

to Rory and Brice Murphy

Norsten

In a corner of the town of Norsten, Minnesota, the railroad tracks used to cut through so that even now with the tracks and trains gone, there is a line of gravel and skunkweed where there used to be ties and steel. Many of the buildings have been torn down and gutted by winter and by tourists needing bits of things for their glass-topped coffee tables, and for that reason the life has gone out of the depot. The building still stands, but the windows are gone. Inside, the benches have been ripped out and the floors made filthy and the walls savaged so the human part is gone. The warm part.

Near the depot there is a false-front tired-white wooden frame store that carries candy bars and cigarettes and expensive packages of food that nobody comes from the farms to buy. The shelves in the store are of planking, clearly temporary, and it looks as if the whole space were designed for something else, rightly so. It used to be a beer hall, known to the farm wives as a saloon, with green-topped tables for the farmers to play cards and drink weak beer when the vicious winters kept them from working. In the back, there is a closed-off room, in which there was once a table and some metal chairs and a clanky projector where the children could watch Gene Autry movies on Saturday night when the men and women came to town. Now it has changed so radically that even the memory is blurred, rippled with time and so different that many of the people who went there do not even count it as part of their lives.

Down the dirt road from the depot are a sagging feed store, a post office, and a brick building that used to be a bank but now houses an army surplus fire engine that is always late for fires. None of this matters except as sadness.

Between the depot and the old store lies a crumbled cement and rock foundation. Charred places and bits of burnt wood are testimony to the fire that leveled the original structure. It is easy to walk past on the split sidewalk without seeing anything of the soul that is still there.

Digging in the foundation area, poking around, brings out bits of steel and iron, old horseshoes, and here and there a plowshare or harness strap. In the corner nearest the road stands a stone and concrete mound with a flattened top. It is almost a piece of sculpture, almost something religious, because the rocks around the edge are worn down and there are marks that can be seen even through the black of the fire damage. After some study, it is clear that the small monument was at one time a forge, that the building was once a blacksmith shop.

It was rare, very rare in this practical farm community because the blacksmith shop never became anything else. The building was put up during the time of horses, those giants in oiled leather harnesses who pulled with a power that snatched men's imaginations. The building was for that time, for the time when men and horses cleared land of forests in ways that can't be thought of without pain or awe; the building was for fashioning new singletrees and doubletrees, was for the hot-flash smell of trip-hammer on the pure steel of plowshares and the stink of hot shoes being fit onto workhorse hooves—fit so they wouldn't pull loose against stumps or underground boulders. The building was for the whine of the crank of the hand-turned bellows and the sweet, hot odor of coal brought to white heat to take the blunted shares. The building was originally made for all these things, but it didn't live into the coming times of repaired auto bodies or the ugly smell of diesel. It committed suicide when a spark from the forge fired the wall and then the roof and finally the rest. Now all that remains are the rocks of the foundation and the edifice of the forge.

It was perhaps proper for the building to kill itself before it had to fit into the new times, before it had to leave its intended purpose. But in a strange way, the suicide was sad. It was sad because if the building had lived, there would be more evidence of the man who worked in it, the man who had it built so he could make heat and steel to fit man and horse. If the building had remained standing, there would now be more of the man who worked the trip-hammer to shape the steel; more of the man who could do whatever it took to tame land that had never been tamed; more of the blacksmith named David who could tame joy and hammer it into the shape of living, the way he hammered steel into the shape of a hoof.

1

<<<<<<<<<<<<<<<<<<<<<<<<<<<<<<<<<<<<<<<<<<<<<<<<<<<<<<

My name is Carley, and I first came to Norsten in high
spring although I didn't know it. I was fourteen and I
didn't know many things, least of all that the people in
Norsten had more than four seasons, had broken them
down into halves, sometimes quarters. I thought it was
the first part of summer, because all the fields were green
except where the rich black of the plowing was new.
There were gulls from the Great Lakes searching the
new dirt for worms and making brilliant white spots in
the jet black of the fields. But it wasn't summer, it was
high spring. This came just before low summer, which

led to high summer and low fall and then middle fall and first freeze—which led to low winter, and high winter, and so on.

But I didn't know all this when I first arrived in Norsten. All I knew was that there were some mosquitoes when I got off the bus in front of the store. I was bitten twice while I waited for the driver to get my big suitcase out of the little bin on the bottom. I was mad and didn't want to be in this small town. I was from Minneapolis and used to a big city. Norsten had a population of maybe two hundred, probably less, and I was there because I had gotten into some trouble and my mother didn't know what else to do with me. I had two uncles in Norsten, and I was to spend the summer with one of them while a judge reviewed my case of vandalism. I suspected neither of my uncles wanted me. They would pick me up outside the store, or were supposed to. It was because they were late that I first met David the way I did.

I put my grip against the front wall of the store and went inside where it was cool. This was not the beer hall, but the old first store that later burned down. It was all dark wood and ordered shelves with sacks of flour and galvanized buckets and straw hats with green visors. I stopped just inside the door to get used to the darkness, and the proprietor looked up from in back of a large roll of butcher paper.

"Can I help you?" He was thin and tall so he looked over you, and I thought he was trying to see if some adults were coming in with me. I did not know that his name was Emil Peterson and that something had happened many years before that kept him from looking people, even young people, in the eyes.

"No. Yes. Do you have any ice cream?" I didn't really want anything, but ice cream sounded good. It was hotting up outside, and I didn't know how long I'd have to wait.

"No cooler. No electricity in town yet." He stared just above my head. "Supposed to come in towards fall, but not yet."

He stopped, and I nodded and moved off to the side, down an aisle, looking at strange mechanical instruments I didn't understand. Horn cutters, castrators, sheep-dip mix, fly-wipe for horses—all together with the food on the other side of the row. I was fully prepared to simply stand and read labels until one of the uncles came to town for me, but the storekeeper was obviously nervous about having me there without buying something. I had been in enough city stores to tell that, had even stolen from some of them. So I turned for the door. "Is it all right for me to leave my suitcase outside?"

He nodded. "Visiting somebody?"

"Staying with relatives for the summer. I'm from Minneapolis." I let some pride come in, big-city snot pride. He didn't reply, and I felt bad as I walked out on the sidewalk. I stood to the side of the door for a moment. The sun was soft, warm, gentle. It would have been nice to stay there, but the mosquitoes came back, and I started to walk.

I headed for the depot because in those days there

were still trains and activity and things to see. Sometimes a big steam-driver with a pulpwood train would come down the tracks and was interesting to watch—clouds of steam, power, *slam-hiss*. The way took me past the blacksmith shop next to the beer hall, where I couldn't go, and that's when I met David.

The shop had a large front door, the kind that pulls up into the ceiling. It was open and there was a smell of horse sweat and coal and burnt hair coming out the door and I stopped. It was impossible not to. The stink would have stopped a truck.

Inside, it was dark, and it took a few seconds for my eyes to find things. Then I saw an immense horse, a giant with brown hair and a white blaze down his face. He was so big—a prehistoric mountain of life, almost a dinosaur—that I had to look up to see into his eyes. He was standing facing me with a placid, contemplative look, and from his left rear hoof, a blue-gray roiling cloud of smoke was working out onto the road.

Holding the hoof up, facing away from me with the huge, hair-draped hoof up between his legs, was a medium-sized man. He was hunched over with his back curved, his knees taking the weight of the horse's back haunch while he held a hot shoe that he'd just hammered to shape to the hoof.

I ducked beneath the cloud a little, and the man sensed movement and turned to see me standing there. He had a round face, with a slightly pug nose, and was probably forty-five, which was old to me then. He had a week-long stubble of beard and an accumulation of black dirt from the forge. When he smiled, the white of his teeth cut the black like a light coming on in a dark room, and the smoke curling up off the hoof between his legs made him look like a happy devil.

"Hello-then." It was almost one word, but pronounced with a thick Norwegian accent so it came out "hello-den"—it was the sort of thing we made jokes about in school. Farmer talk. Country talk. Hick talk. But of course he wasn't kidding, and in any event the accent was so proper on him with the bright blue eyes and the farm cap and the leather apron that it didn't seem funny.

"I didn't mean to interrupt you," I said. "I was just walking by the door and saw the horse and stopped. . . ."

But he had turned back to the hoof. From his apron pocket, he took some nails—he didn't hold them in his mouth, because, I found later, his teeth were bad—and a hammer from a loop on the side and he nailed the shoe on while it was in the right melted-in position. I moved off to the side out of his sight and watched. The nails made a wet sound as they went into and up through the hoof and out the side, where he pulled them over and cut them off with a pair of clippers he had in another loop in his apron. I stood until he was finished and had lowered the hoof and straightened up.

"That's sure a big horse." I wanted to stay and see more, so I thought I had to say something.

"This is old Wheeler," he said. It came out "dis is old Veeler," but high and light so it was pleasant. He

9

slapped the horse on the rump, reaching up to do it. "He's one of a set team belonging to Carl Pederson from out north. The other one is coming in for shoes tomorrow. You're Eunice's kid then?"

The question was tacked on the end so close I nodded without thinking.

"Yes. How did you know that?"

"You look just like her then." He smiled again. "Same eyes and mouth. Work shoulders, just like Eunice." He turned back to the horse, slapped it on the side. Then he walked out front and lifted one of Wheeler's front hooves.

There was a shoe on it, but it was worn badly. I was off to the side where I could see it, and my eyes were getting used to the light. The shoe was all silver, rounded, the cleats almost gone. He used the cutters to snip off the nails on the outside of the hoof, then used a pincer to pull the nails on out the bottom.

The horse tested him, leaned so that his weight was coming down on the lifted leg. David swore lightly. "Never change, do you, Wheeler? Take it up. Take it up." The horse lifted the leg back up.

"Here." He handed me the old shoe, just to make me feel useful, I guess. There was a pile of old shoes in the corner, and he probably just threw them back there. But this one he gave to me, and I held it to the light and looked at it closely. There were cuts in it, actual tiny tears in the steel, where the horse had pulled against rocks.

"Old shoes are always prettier," he said, working on

the hoof with a rasp without looking up. "Soft. Shaped. Sometimes I hang them on the wall and look at them."

He finished the hoof and let it down, then went over to his forge where there was a keg of new shoes. They weren't in any order and he fished until he got one about right, going just by his eyes, and this he took back to the horse and held it against the raised and filed hoof. The shoe was too wide across, and he put it on the anvil, thumping it lightly with a medium hammer to pinch it closed a little. Then he tried the hoof again, and the shoe was the right size. He went back to the forge.

"Crank." He motioned with his chin to the crank on the bellows on the wall, a wooden-handled steel blower that fed an air pipe into the forge. There was already hot coal fired in the basin—a stone fire basin two feet across, surrounded by tools on a steel rod, all waist high. When I turned the handle, the bellows made a whine, low at first and then higher and higher as the gears caught speed and the air went through the pipe into the bottom of the fire basin with a dull roar.

The coals had been warm gray, almost black, and they now went to soft red and then brighter and at last to white. I stared at them until the heat came up into my face making my eyes water. I moved off, but kept cranking.

David worked the steel shoe down into the coals with a pair of tongs, covering all the bare metal with hot coals until the horseshoe nestled in the white heat.

"How's your mother then?"

I looked up from the fire. For a moment I'd forgotten

where I was and why. "She's fine. Do you know her?"

He nodded. "She's my sister. I'm your Uncle David."

I started. "But . . . but I thought somebody was coming to the store to get me. I mean, an uncle was supposed to meet me. . . ." I went back to staring at the fire. The shoe was already taking the heat, and where he brushed it open with his tongs, I could see the steel glowing red.

"There was nineteen children in the Hansen family." Hansen was my mother's maiden name. "You got lots of uncles and aunts. I'm just one of them then. Hansens is everywhere, just everywhere up here in the north." Now he pulled the shoe out of the fire. It was white-red and cooling fast, and he moved over to the anvil and took the medium hammer out of the rack on the anvil stand.

Just light taps, nothing to change the shape much. Almost kisses. Small sparks falling out and away as he turned and tapped the shoe. Then back to the horse, where he raised the hoof with one hand while holding the tongs with another.

He placed the shoe against the hoof. Boiling clouds of blue smoke came up, stinking thick, and he pulled the shoe away to let it cool. He touched again, pulled away again, letting it get cooler and cooler and fitting it each time. Then he hammered in the nails, setting and seating the cool shoe, bending the nails over and cutting them off. All the time the horse just stood, waiting, staring out the door into the afternoon. Flies and mosquitoes were on him in clouds. His skin jiggled to keep them off, but there was peace in his eyes. I wondered what he was thinking, because it was clear from his look that he was thinking something.

"You are going to stay with either Harvey or me," David said, straightening. He leaned for a moment against the horse, resting, and I could now see rivulets of sweat working down the black of his face, cutting white lines in it. "We wasn't sure which, because we heard you was coltish and a little wild. Are you?"

I didn't answer, thinking, still looking at the horse. "No. I don't think so. I got in some trouble is all. But it's done now, I think."

He nodded. "That's the way I had it figured. So why don't you stay with me, and we'll see what happens?"

I went back out for my suitcase and brought it into the shop and put it in the corner out of the way. I spent the rest of the afternoon into early evening helping David in the blacksmith shop, working the flywheel that ran the trip-hammer while he *ping ping slam*'d the hot plowshares out to a sharp edge. And that is how I came to know David all in fire and heat and the ringing of steel and the smell of thick smoke.

2

<<<<<<<<<<<<<<<<<<<<<<<<<<<<<<<<<<<<<<<<<<<<<<<<<<<<<<<

At the end of the day, I was all sweat and stink, and
David closed down the forge with a kind of tired, sad
smile that was on the edge of being happy.

"We quit now," he said, looking down at me.

In back of the blacksmith shop stood a wagon. It was
a work wagon, the kind they call a buckboard in the cow-
boy movies. There was a shed next to the wagon, and
David brought two horses in harness out of the shed.

They came out like old friends, moving over the long
wooden tongue of the wagon in a slow dance. Legs moving, big black legs on two black horses, big as two walls,

moving gently with David's burned-dark hands until they stood in place in front of the wagon.

David hooked the trace chains to the singletrees and helped me throw my suitcase in the back. Actually it wasn't a suitcase, but a kind of fancy cardboard box with stripes, so it looked like more than it really was.

Then we got up in the wagon, and he said some gentle words to the horses. By the time we hit the street, I had transformed the wagon into an overland stage and my suitcase into a valuable cargo. The fantasy lasted until we reached the edge of town sitting up over the high wheels, looking down on everything from the top of the spring seat.

"It's two miles to home," he said, pulling the team left on a gravel road just east of the depot. "Nice ride in summer. Sometimes I walk." He was cutting his words as if he didn't want to talk. I felt the same way. It was such a beautiful evening, with the air soft as a warm blanket and the wagon just pulling along with little creaks and groans and the *smell-scrub* of the harness pulling, that talking seemed a waste.

The road was fairly smooth. A horse-drawn grader had evened it down from the ruts of spring thaw. The ditches had standing water, and now and again a set of mallards would get up, flying ahead of us to land in the ditch up a ways until we came on them again. The woods back of the fields were a deep bright green that made me think of pictures I'd seen of Ireland in a *National Geographic Magazine.* It was all so different from where I lived, from Minneapolis, that I was hard put to take it

15

all in. This was where my mother was born, and the people I would meet were supposed to be my family, but I knew nothing of them, nothing of this country. I didn't even know their names. We had never talked of them at home, partly because my father was from Kansas and didn't like the woods up north and partly because my mother had left the farm early and gone away to the city. Their life was so involved that they seldom talked of up north.

I was from the gray city with its alleys of trash and rusted iron and hidden places in back of billboards. It was all hard edges and brittle talk—all city stone and noise and light that didn't go away at night, but flashed dull and blue in the windows, over and over. I was from a place where even when some green plant did show, it was covered with a film of dust.

And here, on this ride from the blacksmith shop down two miles of country road to David's home I was besieged by such color, such richness and fullness and thickness, that I became almost ill with it—the way you become ill from eating too many éclairs, too much pastry. My throat closed with it, my mind closed with it, so that I had to look out over the horses and down the road, just across the shiny black backs at the gravel until my mind could take it all in.

David was watching me, and he laughed. "Pretty much, ain't it then? And if you think this is something, wait'll you see fall. Color just *blows* at you. Gets so you gotta close your eyes every so often to catch up."

I nodded, but didn't say anything—my throat was

still a little tight—and we rode a full half mile with just the sounds of the wagon, the harness, and the horses coming up around us. Even those sounds were rich—creaks of oiled leather, fat with grease and shiny with copper rivets; shuffles and rubs of old, worn, fitted wood that made groans of music; jingles coming up from the trace chains; and the muffled *flit-OP*, *flit-OP* of the hooves in the gravel.

It made a feeling, all of it, as if there could never be anything wrong or ugly in the world. That is not an easy thing to accept. And here it all was, around and through me. It was all I could do to stay on the wagon seat and not jump out, run back to town, and take the next bus back home because this, this was so much.

But I stayed and the feeling passed, worked off as the country came in. When we'd gone a mile and a half, David nudged ahead with his chin and said "Home." I looked down the road, and in the distance, on the left, I could see a white frame house and to the left of that, a large red barn.

As we got closer, I could see some cows against the green pasture in back of the barn—bright black-and-white slabs of color (Holsteins, I later learned). I could also see that the farm had a general run-down appearance. Not falling apart, but a well-used look. The farm made me think of old leather, used and warm but strong. As we got closer still, I could see what looked like a mob of kids running all over the place.

"Last count there was seven of them," David said, reading my eyes. "Should be more but two didn't make it and one's grown and gone into the navy. Of course, he writes. We get a letter every month. He's on a carrier in the Pacific, but the letters come regular and that's nice for Emily. That's your aunt's name." Abruptly he stopped talking as the wagon hit a chuckhole. "New one. Damn gophers. They gut the road underneath, and the water comes into the holes and freezes and then busts holes out. Ha *bah!*" It was a snort-laugh, so sudden that at first I supposed it was a command to the horses. I didn't know that he'd thought of something funny, some picture. Then he chuckled privately and turned to me. "Back—I think it was in '17 or '18—a slicker come through here selling cars. I think they was Maxwells, but they could have been something else."

He paused to use the reins to slap at the flies on the horses, slow and loose and easy, so they knew it wasn't a demand for speed. We were going by a small slough. The deerflies came up in a swarm, and the horses' skin wriggled like fur-covered jelly. Welts appeared as if by magic.

"My pa, that would be your grandpa, was alive and crowing in the roost then, and I tell you there wasn't nothing like him for quiet. He was thin, but slab-leather tough. He never talked, and he worked a team of Belgiums that made the ground shake. I *saw* them pop stumps bigger than my waist and without cutting the roots—just like rotten teeth. And he didn't like engines at all. Not at all. So here comes this slicker to sell him this Maxwell, and don't you know he talked Pa into going for a ride down the road. Pa wouldn't let us kids go even though we all wanted to. But he got in, got in while that fellow started it up, all pops and snorts. The slicker climbs in, and off they go down the road, smoke and noise just blowing. Just blowing."

Another slap with the reins, a soft tongue-cheek sound to let the horses know he was paying attention. The cloud of flies rose on their backs and resettled, and I wondered how they could stand it. They were covered with bites by this time, and I was finding that a deerfly bite felt like a hot needle being inserted into an open wound.

"Pa never figured to see us again," he continued. "By the time he cleared the yard and hit the old road, he was pretty sure he was a goner. Pa told us later when that slicker souped that Maxwell up to speed, it was like the fence posts had turned into netting, they moved so fast. Then . . ."

He stopped to laugh and reached over and slapped me on the leg so hard it stung. I winced and rubbed. It felt like getting slapped with a piece of dried leather.

". . . then they hit a chuckhole and the left front wheel of the Maxwell came off and went down the road on its own. Ha-*hah*. Maxwell, slicker, and Pa went into a ditch full of water like shot ducks and Pa, he was so mad that he wouldn't give the slicker a team to pull the car out. It set there a week until he hired a team from town." He snugged back on the lines a bit. "Hold it there, you damn fools. We ain't home yet."

The horses jerked at the traces, tight little jumps, their bellies tightening up in rippling muscle lurches;

the yard was only a quarter mile away now and they wanted to get in, get home. They were pulling harder all the time. In just a few seconds, the reins were so tight they looked like stretched wire across the horses' backs. There was a power from them coming up through the lines into David's hands, almost a hum of power that just worked up off their shoulders into the lines and back up to his hands. I'd never seen anything like it. In an instant the team had gone from plodding down the road, scuffing along, to being a force that was alive, a force that turned the team and the lines and David and the wagon into a single entity.

Four hundred yards from the gate or perhaps a bit less, the team broke into a trot, and I grabbed the seat as the wagon increased speed. Fifty yards later, they broke into a tightly controlled canter, and within ten more yards, it was a full out gallop, the iron wheels on the wagon screeching and my breath gone, as the team tore for the driveway and home.

David was standing now, leaning back against the slam-pull of the driving shoulders of the team, piling out and down and forward like hair-covered engines. I couldn't do anything but hang on to the side of the seat as the wagon thundered down the road and the team turned sharply into the driveway.

The wagon followed the tongue and started to roll. It would have rolled over too, but there was loose gravel that allowed the wheels to slide sideways to take the strain. The wagon whipped left, then right, and settled in back of the horses as they roared down the driveway into the yard followed by a steady stream of ripping

20

swearing from David, who was now standing up and leaning back against the lines with his full weight.

I had one mental flash of kids, geese, dogs, and a hundred or so chickens going every which way. Then I closed my eyes as David pulled on the right rein and wheeled the team around in a great circle in the yard. They stopped, heaving at the sides, sweat popping out on them like instant black rivers; stopped to stand on electric legs that jerked and popped with fire to run still more; stopped while David eased down on the reins and tied them off to the side of the seat and got down. He walked around the horses, slapping them gently on the rumps and sides, and then began unhooking the trace chains.

"G'damn horses, got no sense. What's the matter with you running that way, blowing yourselves all out—G'damn horses anyway. . . ." It was a kind of song, or perhaps chant would be a better word. As he unhooked them, they relaxed and settled—you could see their skin quiet down. Then he led them off to the barn.

I was still sitting on the seat, frozen in fear, and I began to feel self-conscious. With David and the horses gone to the barn, I was alone, the wagon still, and the animals and kids that had moved away in panic began to drift back. Even the chickens came, so that in a moment there was a circle of staring faces, animal and human—the human faces deeply dirty—all around the front of the wagon, all looking up at me except for the chickens, who were busily inspecting the new manure left by the horses.

"Hi." I tried a smile, but none of them responded except to look down shyly and then back up. There were six or seven of them (it was hard to count in the pack of people and animals), and they were from ages twelve or so and down. The two young ones, perhaps three and four, were blond—everybody was some shade of blond—and it was impossible to determine which sex they were. They both had runny noses and stared at me with frankness. After a moment, the smallest one came up to the wagon, climbed the wheel, and looked over the edge of the high seat at me.

"Are you mean?" It was a straight question, but before I could answer, she or he went on. "We heard you was mean, that's what we heard. We heard you was mean, and we wasn't to have nothing to do with you until we made sure if you was really mean. Are you mean?"

"Lynette!" A boy came up and snaked her off the wagon wheel with one hand, dragging her back to the circle of waiting faces.

"Lynette talks too much," he said up to me, though he couldn't hold my eyes for shyness. "She always did. You're supposed to get the corner upstairs, so if you come, I'll show you where you're gonna sleep."

Glad of the chance to move, I jumped in back and got my suitcase and followed the boy, still without knowing his name. Later, I found out it was Tinker. That was his nickname; I never heard his given name.

Inside the house I was hit by smells again, only this time pleasant smells and not shop stink. Baking bread, cooking potatoes, and frying meat on a wood range; sharp tang of burning birch in the stove, coffee from a pot. We passed through a kitchen full of rich steam smells. A young woman was working bread dough on a side counter while an older woman—my Aunt Emily—turned meat frying in a huge cast-iron griddle on the wood range. The stove was a giant of nickel steel shined to brilliance, with a clean steel top and black iron burners. It dwarfed Emily when she turned to look at me, fork poised, flour on her arms from dusting the meat. She was thin and there were some hairs loose from her bun in back, loose and down to the sides, but it didn't look messy at all.

Emily smiled. "Dinner soon. Put your stuff upstairs, and come back down to wash up."

I nodded and followed Tinker up a curving, narrow stairway in back of the stove. It cut back twice and came out in a large, single upstairs room, bare under the rafters, except for bunks down the side like in a barracks. Back in one corner, a bed had a rolled-up feather tick on it, and Tinker took me to it.

"This is yours." He talked like David—"dis iss yourss"—but I was rapidly getting used to the Norwegian accent. "Girls sleep in the other end of the room, and there's a blanket across for privacy." He sounded proud, and I wondered why. Then he added, "I hung the blanket. Seemed like a good thing to do since we are growing up."

I nodded again. Actually I was stunned, totally taken aback by the stark poverty of it all. Back home, I had a single room, a bed with a real mattress, walls with pictures.

Here the walls were rafters. There were bunks with

23

people close on all sides, beds made of raw wood with ropes for the bottom, no place to put my stuff, no privacy at all. The mattresses were crudely sewn and the clothes on all the kids had a catch-it-in-the-middle-hand-me-down look. The cheer and rich smells and sounds were not enough anymore. I sat on the corner bunk and pushed the suitcase in under the frame. Then I put my face in my hands and fought back crying.

I felt alone. Before, there had been bad times, especially when I was mean—as Lynette put it—bad times when I could not fit into the world, when I would not be part of other people and would act crazy and do things with no sense in them. There was a garage that I had burned down, a two-car garage next to where I lived in the city. I burned it down because there were matches and gasoline in a can, and for no other reason. Afterward a man came and talked to my mother. Police were with him. There was no sense to what I had done, nothing that could be found to justify it. I felt only remorse and pain and shame as I cried. My mother looked like she was in shock.

That was terrible. A terrible bad time when I sat alone in my room and stared at the walls and thought I might be a maniac and should be gone.

Again there came a bad time when I threw rocks through the stained glass window of a church two blocks from my home. There was no thought in it, only the action. The stupid action and then the coming of the minister and again the police. Then the crying and the shame once more and the room—God, the walls of the room all around and me alone.

There were many bad times like that. Many times when the police came and finally the worst bad time, the time when we had to talk to the judge, who asked me the same question I had asked myself again and again—why I acted the way I acted.

I couldn't answer him, because I didn't know.

But here in my uncle's house, I was not just alone and asking myself why I was a maniac, I was in a whole strange world where nobody could or would understand me. Where there wasn't even electricity and where they talked funny. I was not just bad, I was different. This was all different, and there was only poverty and shame.

I sat on the edge of the bed and wouldn't go downstairs, couldn't go downstairs and that is how I missed dinner, sitting in the dark, with no electricity and no lights.

Then David came upstairs.

3

<<<<<<<<<<<<<<<<<<<<<<<<<<<<<<<<<<<<<<<<<<<<<<

"Emily's got a plate saved for you downstairs," he said, sitting on the small cot next to me. "It's on the back of the stove keeping warm."

"I can't eat." He smelled different now. Smelled of barn and something else—soap. Lye soap. His hand touched my shoulder. His hand was hard, but at the same time it wasn't hard. "I'm sorry. I can't eat."

"You've got to eat, sorry or not. If you don't eat, you won't have nothing to burn tomorrow to keep you going." The hand tousled my hair. "Nothing is like it first seems. You come down and eat, and don't worry. Everything will be all right."

26

His voice had the same sound it had when he had talked to the horses, the same kind of gentle edge to it, and I realized that I would have to go downstairs sooner or later. I stood up.

"Good," he said, standing with me. "We'll go down together."

The kitchen was still warm with the heat from the stove and thick with the smell of food. Emily put a plate on the table when she saw me coming down. It was heaped with fried potatoes and chunks of some kind of meat. She poured a big glass of thick milk from a large jar she pulled out of a hole under the kitchen sink down along the well pipe. There was enough food for four of me, more than I could ever eat, but I sat down and started. David sat on the other side of the table and filled a pipe with tobacco, packing it with his round fingers, jamming the tobacco down carefully. He lit it with a wooden match he scratched under the table, puffed and filled his cheeks with smoke, then let it out in a blue cloud that went up into the white light of the Coleman lantern.

I noticed that there were no kids in the room. Not even the older daughter who had been helping Emily with the meal when I arrived. Just Emily, David, and me.

He let smoke out. "Mebbe it is that you don't like us then?"

I had a mouthful of meat, and I pushed it over to the side with my tongue. "What do you mean?"

"If you don't like us, mebbe we should work out something else. Mebbe you could go to Harvey's place."

"No. I mean, I like you fine. It's just that it's all so . . . so different." I was scared, and I thought, *You are so*

27

poor and this is all so far from how I usually live. I didn't say it, of course. "I won't act that way anymore. I'm over it now."

David studied me through the pipe smoke. He didn't stare, just looked. Then a strange thing happened. He turned his face from me and said to Emily, "I think Bets is going to calf tomorrow. She didn't come in tonight. We should find her and get her home, so we don't lose the calf to wolves when it comes."

This must have been some kind of signal, because the door slammed open and kids started streaming in. They began doing things, and the kitchen was filled with noise and movement. It was like I had always been there. Nobody even looked at me while I finished eating. I not only cleaned my plate but wolfed down a piece of fresh rhubarb pie to boot. I must have been hungrier than I thought or else the food was awfully good, because when Emily put another piece of pie down in front of me, I made that disappear as well.

It was late when I finished eating, and I thought we'd all go to bed. Instead, everything got quiet and the kids grabbed pieces of wood from the woodbox to sit on. Emily filled her cup with coffee from the back of the stove, poured a cup for David, and sat at the table. She took some sewing out of a basket and went to work on it. Sitting there bent over the cloth, she made a curve in the light. The kids sat around the table on the cutoff pieces of stovewood. I thought maybe they were going to pray or something, it was so quiet. But I was wrong.

David relighted his pipe and took a long series of

28

puffs, then cleared his throat with a swallow of the coffee.

"It come a time in late winter back when I was first working the woods that a surprise storm come in. It snowed mebbe two feet or more, and then the temperature dropped to forty, fifty below. God, it was cold. We was in the woods up north, on the edge of Canada and mebbe over the border sometimes, and it was so cold we had horses freeze, standing dead in the back of the dray barn, standing dead and frozen like they was carved from hairy ice."

Everybody was listening now. The room was warm with the high spring night and the hiss of the lantern burning and the sound of the bugs hitting the screens, but I could feel and smell the cold he was talking about. Blue cold.

"We was cutting wood for the paper companies," David said after a moment, "and that was a day we thought we wouldn't work. But those big companies only paid for wood we brought out, so the men went to work. You never *saw* so many busted axes and bucksaws. They'd bind in the cold. You'd give a little twist, and ping, there'd go your saw or axe. Steel can't take hard cold, true cold like that—it gets as brittle as glass."

Again he paused and got the pipe going once more, and I saw in the faces of the kids that he wasn't through yet. I also could tell that this wasn't normal, staying up late and hearing a story of the way it used to be. By now, it was going on eleven by the kitchen clock, and I found later that was way past their usual bedtime.

29

"There was an old guy named Johnny Peterson back then, really old. He'd come from the old country. He didn't work, of course. He was too old. But he lived in a cabin back in the woods, and during that cold time he smelled death coming to him."

It got even more quiet then. It was so still in the room that Emily even stopped her sewing, looking right at David.

"Johnny, he was always one to make you laugh. He was so big when he was young that he couldn't get no clothes to fit him, and he was always playing jokes on people. Once, I heard, when he was cutting wood, the foreman was in the toilet and Johnny dropped a grandpa white pine—four feet across it was—so it blocked the door of the toilet. It took them six hours to saw that log out of there with bucksaws, and that foreman was spitting and cussing the whole time.

"So Johnny, he was old, and he smelled death coming, but he wanted to play just one more joke on the men he used to work with." David stopped for more coffee. Emily signed with a wrist, and one of the daughters filled his empty cup from the pot on the stove. "Johnny opened the door of the cabin and laid down on the floor and spread his arms and legs out as wide as he could get them, and he died like that. All alone in the woods, in that small cabin, spread out like the spokes on a giant wheel. Ha!" He laughed and slapped my leg again like he had on the wagon, so hard it cracked. "They didn't find him dead for three days, and when they did, he was frozen solid. Just like a rock. Frozen on his back, all spread out with a big grin on his face. I tell you, that was something to see. When the foreman took us in to get the body, it was hard not to laugh."

He stopped again, and for a minute I thought that was the end of the story. In fact, I was just thinking I liked the one about the car better. But then he widened his smile and showed his teeth. "But that wasn't the joke. Even dying funny wasn't enough for Johnny. No, that Johnny Peterson had to have more. See, the way he was spread out and frozen like that, you couldn't work him through the small door of the cabin. That was the joke. There was six of us with axes and we had to chop for two hours in that cold, breaking axes and swearing, with him laying on the floor looking up at us with a big grin on his face—two hours to chop the wall out of the cabin to make a hole big enough to get him out and loaded on a dray. Ahh, that Johnny—he was something. He was something." He put his pipe on the table. "And now to bed. It'll be hard tomorrow, and we need sleep."

So we all went upstairs to bed, and I was all in under the blanket and half asleep before I realized that I hadn't felt afraid or lonely. It was like I'd lived there all my life. I just clomped up the stairs, peeled in the dark, and climbed into bed. I said good-night to the other boys in the room and pressed my head back into the pillow.

Just as my brain was turning over, I thought of how it had happened. Thought that David had made it happen by keeping us up late and telling us the story of Johnny Peterson and his last joke. David had made me part of the family.

"Tinker," I whispered down the room through the dark. "Are you still awake?"

"Sure. What do you want?"

"Does he always tell stories like that?"

"No. Not always. Only when he wants to."

"It was a good story."

"Yes. They always are."

"Good night, Tinker."

"Good night. Tomorrow I'll take you with me to help find Bets."

"Sure. I'd like that."

Then just the sound of the bugs outside and the whine of mosquitoes trying to get through the screen and, finally, sleep.

4

Parts of those first two weeks at David's farm mix with other parts, some of them good, some not so good, and finally a very bad part. But, in memory, they are all mixed into a painting with soft edges, so that even the bad parts have a kind of beauty.

Maybe that was what David meant when he said later—much later—that it was like looking at something you didn't like and making your eyes blur so you couldn't see it, but I don't think so.

Like that first morning. It must have been midnight before we finally got to sleep after hearing the story of

Johnny Peterson, but at first light, which cracks about four in the morning in the north at that time of year, David's voice boomed up the stairwell.

"Up, *up* now! Dark is for sleep, light is for life. *Up* now!"

I hadn't been up at that hour ever in my life that I could remember. But there was something in his voice that made you want to see the day. A kind of song or something.

Tired or not, my feet hit the floor before I knew it, and I put my pants on and stood up. I could see Tinker in the gray of the dawn coming in the window as he pulled his pants on with a *whoosh* that came from the heavy canvas Emily used in making them.

"Don't pull on your shirt yet," Tinker said.

"Why not?"

"Because you'll just have to take it off again to do the bucket. Come on."

He made for the stairs, and I followed, trying to match his clumps down two at a time, with two small boys behind. One was four and the other six.

The kitchen was already alive. Heat and the smell of cooking meat and potatoes and eggs and coffee came from the stove. David sat at the table rubbing sleep out of his eyes. Because it wasn't quite daylight, he had lighted a small oil lamp on the table, which gave everything a yellow glow. The girls weren't down yet, and I headed for a chair, but Tinker kept on going out the door and waved for me to follow.

Outside he went to the stock tank by the barn and

took down a small pail, the kind I later found were used for feeding calves.

"Lean over the tank," he said, filling the bucket. "Then you can do me."

I put my head over the tank, and he hit me with about three gallons of night-chilled water, poured it over my head and shoulders. Some of it trickled down my back and went into my jeans, and I was awake, awake and tossing my head the way the colts did in the morning, jumping in a little circle in the new sun.

Then I poured it over Tinker and we took turns with the two small boys, sloshing them heavily because, as Tinker said, "They ain't dirt-broke yet, and it builds in their hair."

We combed with our fingers, dried our faces with the air, and went back into the kitchen, where we ate breakfast with our T-shirts sticking to us in places.

"See to Bets after we harness," David said after breakfast and went out lighting his pipe. Tinker ran after him, and I realized that I was supposed to follow.

It was light outside now. Light with heat coming for the day, and we all went to the barn where David opened the back door and called to the cattle just once with a low "boss."

They filed in—six milk cows, all black-and-white, their udders swollen with milk. David slapped each of them lightly on the rump as they passed him standing in the door. They all knew where to go and stood in their stanchions while Tinker went down the line and locked the metal neckholders in place. Then Emily came from the house with the oldest daughter, Emma, and they started to milk.

David called the team of horses into the barn from the pasture and gave them some oats. Then he started harnessing them. He put the collars around their necks first, buckling them and settling them back against their shoulders, leather to muscle and all the time talking and making soft sounds. I was standing there watching because there wasn't anything I knew how to do. I would probably have stayed except that Tinker hit my arm lightly.

"Come on. We've got to find Bets."

He went out across the mud and manure in back of the barn, barefoot, squishing it up through his toes. I followed in my tennis shoes, trying to miss the worst parts.

The grass in the pasture was wet green and heavy with dew, and my feet were soaked in no time at all. But it was warm now, and the wet feet didn't feel bad.

We found Bets back in the corner of the pasture, half a mile or so from the barn. She was a great slab of a cow, black-and-white like the rest, but thin. She'd already had her calf. It was on the ground, warm and wet and shiny, raising and lowering its head while she licked the hair dry and kept nudging it with her muzzle to get it up. I thought I'd never seen anything so pretty. The cow and the calf were soft morning and the way they stood, back in a corner of green willows almost like a little church, was a part of that high spring that still makes me wonder if it was real.

Bets raised her head when we came, brought the horn

36

around in a gentle curve to protect her calf. When she saw it was us, she let her neck back down to the calf, licking it alive.

"It's a bull calf," Tinker said, his voice a whisper. "A little bull calf. Ain't he slick? June calves are always slick."

Slick was a good word for it and for the time we spent waiting for her to finish cleaning the calf and get it up and walking. It didn't take more than half an hour before she had him on his feet looking for his milk. Then she started for the barn, turning back and nudging the calf along. We walked behind them, brushing flies and mosquitoes away, not talking, just moving with the smell of the calf coming back on us wet and new in the morning.

I was tired from being up half the night, and my eyes burned. By the time we got back to the barn with Bets and her new bull calf, I felt I was in a dream, fuzzy around the edges—happy, but a little silly, too. I didn't think of the city anymore, but just the morning and where I was and that was nice.

We sat out by the barn most of that day after we got Bets in, and Tinker told me about the family. That was part of the blurred picture of those first two weeks as well—Tinker sitting down along the barn wall with a straw jammed in the corner of his mouth, his hair blond and shining in the sun, while I leaned back against the wall and went in and out of almost dozing.

"We are four boys and four girls," he said. "Exact. My older brother Larry, he's in the navy on a carrier in the Pacific fighting in the war, and we get letters sometimes that Pa reads at night to all of us. He's something, Larry is—those letters are good ones."

I nodded, let the sun work into my face.

"He's nineteen, Larry is, and I'm nine and the other two boys—Kipper and Wes—they're six and four. Then the girls are sort of the same. Emma is the oldest, and she's eighteen and got a whale of a crush on Dwayne Morvig who lives down the road and doesn't come around much because he's thinking of the army. Then the other three girls are twelve, ten, and three and they're named Patty, Wanda, and Lynette."

"How do you keep them all straight?" I asked without opening my eyes. "When I first came yesterday, it seemed like there were kids all over the place."

"It's easy when you go by clothes," he said. "You just remember who's wearing the clothes from the one before, and you can keep them straight. That's what I do."

"Clothes?"

"Sure. See, we don't have money. We never have money. Even when Pa works hard in the spring with the plowshares and implements and he's supposed to get money for it, he doesn't. They all pay in food and grain. All we have is milk and cream money, and that's not much. So we have to make clothes wear from one kid down to the next. Kipper, he wears mine until he grows too much, and then he hands them down to Wes. There's a bunch of Larry's clothes waiting for me when I get bigger. So you just go by the clothes."

I laughed. "That's a good way to go."

"Sure. If there's a big pile of dust and a fight going

38

on in the middle of the calves or sheep or chickens and I reach in and pull out somebody wearing my old striped T-shirt, I know it's Kipper, because Wes wouldn't be wearing the shirt yet. It's easy."

Heat and dust and clothes and kids and animals—those were the first two weeks at David's farm, all blended together in warm sun and lazy times.

There was a small river, and we went fishing for bullheads the third or fourth night. Tinker took me down to the bank after dark one night, and we made a fire to smoke away the bugs. We baited hooks with worms and let them lie on the bottom in the black, slow water.

We didn't talk, but sat staring into the fire and watched the sparks climb into the night and felt the lines until the fish started biting. I had never fished for bullheads before, never caught the ugly little whiskered bottom feeders, and Tinker had to show me how to wait past the first bite. I missed a couple until he showed me how to ease the worm down to them, let them swallow it, then pull them in.

He also showed me in the light of the fire how to grab so their spines wouldn't go into my hands and leave the swollen hole that makes your hands hurt for days. When we had fifty bullheads and it was close to the middle of the night, we stopped and went home and dropped them in the stock tank to clean the next day. Even that, cleaning them, was a kind of beautiful part of the picture of those first two weeks.

We sat on milkstools outside the barn and cut them down the middle with a sharp knife and dropped the guts, glistening and gray-red on the ground, and laughed as the barn cats fought the chickens for them, pulling and tugging. Then we used pliers to snip off the spines and peel the skin off. Later, when Emily fried them in bear grease and served them with thin fried potatoes, I wished we'd caught more than fifty.

Tinker also showed me all about milking. Every morning and every night, the cows filed into the barn and took their stanchions. Emily and the girls milked them, because David was at the blacksmith shop in town. We took turns cranking the separator, which pulled the cream out of the milk in a high-pitched spin-whine. When the cows were all milked, stripped out, and let go, we cleaned the gutters with shovels, throwing the manure, all steaming thick-rich-stink, out in back of the barn, where David would pick it up once a month to spread it on the fields. Once Tinker took some milk from Bets straight into a glass and held it out for me. When I tasted it, it was still hot from her heat. It was not sweet but something like it, and you could smell her hair in the heat of the milk and smell the calf, too. It was good and not so good at the same time, but very rich, and I wondered what they did to city milk to ruin it the way they did, make it thin and soupy.

Tinker showed me as much as he could in those first weeks, showed me the way of the farm and his life and how his family lived. As he said, they had no money—I never actually saw any coins or cash—yet they didn't seem to want any, either. I had never seen anybody who was so poor, not even in the bad parts of Minneapolis where we used to ride our bikes down the street knowing that we couldn't stop, couldn't get off or we'd be in trouble; not in the alleys in the backs of the bars was it as poor in money as it was at David's farm. Even during the worst times, my mother always had a dime or a quarter.

David's family had no money. I didn't understand how that could be until I'd been there over a week and was digging in my pocket for something and pulled out a dollar bill that was crammed down in the corner. It had been there all the time, wadded and tight and small, and I took it out and looked at it and wondered what I could do with it. Mother had given it to me when I came north, and I had forgotten it. After a moment, I crammed it back down in the pocket and forgot about it again.

Nine years old to my fourteen, Tinker showed me things I had never dreamed could be, a way of living I couldn't believe at first. Soon I was living the same way—running barefoot through the dust and mud, cleaning fish, tanning in the sun—a way of living that boiled down to just one word, *happiness*.

Tinker took me inside his world. That's why when I went crazy with rage and did what I did, it was so bad. It wasn't that I just did something bad, which I did, or that I really hurt him—I didn't. It was an act of stupidity, of anger. It was something wild and ugly in me that came out—that's why I spent the rest of the summer at the blacksmith shop helping David and learning how to hammer joy into my life.

5

‹‹

In back of the barn, David had a large pen in which he kept the yearling calves. If they were let run, they would nurse from the cows in the pasture and dry them out before the regular milking times in the mornings and nights.

"The calves are all spicy," Tinker said one morning, "because they don't get to run during the day. That's why it's so much fun to play rodeo. You want to try it?"

I'd been there two weeks, two weeks and a little more, at that time. We had fished and played, and I had been given certain chores to perform. I was to work alone on the separator and clean the barn while Tinker fed the calves. I was part of it all now, and the city was getting out of me, and I thought that it would be good to learn to ride the calves. I had ridden the workhorses once, sat up on each of the great flat tables of flesh, plodding down the road. Even when they trotted, I stayed on, and it didn't seem that difficult.

"Sure. Let's ride the calves."

Of course, it wasn't that quick and easy. The calves, as Tinker had said, were full of vinegar. They weren't about to have two barefoot, half-naked summer savages climb on and go for a ride.

And they weren't small, either. A yearling Holstein steer is as big as a small pony, and a lot stringier and tougher to handle. He has a long shoulder with a sharp top ridge, and he can spin on a dime. Just getting one into position to ride is a job.

First we used some old boards to make a kind of chute next to the gate of the pen. We braced it so that when the gate was opened, it also opened the front end of the chute.

The calves watched us working with wary eyes, as if they had an idea that we were up to no good. And certainly all the hammering and slamming going on at the end of their pen didn't help them settle down any.

When at last the chute was done, the noise had attracted an audience, and the rest of the children—except for Emma—came to watch. With a great deal of jumping and dodging back and forth, we finally got a calf in the chute. By this time, I was having second thoughts. There

was a wild look in the calf's eyes, with some white show-
ing, and you could see his muscles quivering and shaking
under the skin like something hot and alive and mean.

Tinker looked at me. "You want to go first?"

I shook my head. "No. You do the first one. I'll just
watch and see how it's done."

Tinker climbed the fence next to the calf. "When I
swing on, you open the gate, and I'll ride him out into
the pasture."

I jumped around to the gate and got ready. Tinker
scampered over the fence onto the back of the calf,
grabbed a handful of the loose skin on top of the calf's
neck, and gave the word through gritted teeth. "Open
her up!"

I slammed open the gate, and the effect was immedi-
ate. The calf, driven by all the pent-up energy of having
been closed up for months, shot out of the chute like a
huge, fur-covered cannonball. With a low, guttural
"merff," he didn't hit the ground for ten feet, and then
he merely bunched and flew again, trying to shake the
sticky little rider off his back.

For a second or two, it looked like Tinker would
make it. Eyes shut tight, both hands full of calf, he hung
in the middle of the animal for three or four jumps. Then
the calf went north, and he went south, end over end,
to land in a rumpled heap in the dirt thirty feet out from
the pen.

The kids cheered wildly, and I went over to help him
up, but he brushed my hand away. "Don't fret—I'm all
right. I would have stayed on if I'd had something to
hang on to. To do this right, we need a rope."

44

Before I could stop him, he'd gone for a rope, and I was cornered. To be honest, the last thing in the world I wanted was to climb up on one of those calves and ride him out. Especially now that I had seen one of them in action. It was about like riding a bomb.

But there it was—I was caught, flat and down caught. Tinker had done it, and he was only nine. Plus he had done it the hard way, without a rope. I had to do it now, like it or not, and I could feel fear in my throat and in back of my eyes. Fear and something else—something I couldn't name, something not good. Something ugly.

Tinker came back with the rope, and he was smiling. "You ought to get a good ride. They're *really* cranked up now—with a rope you'll be able to hang on longer." He studied me. "That's if you still want to go."

I tried to smile, but I didn't feel it. "Sure. I'm all for it."

Again we scampered around and finally got a calf in the chute. He was bigger than the one before, and his eyes were rolling back in his head. There was spit hanging down from the corner of his mouth and one nostril. I thought I would die if I rode him, die and be stomped into jelly.

"Help me with the rope," Tinker called from across the chute. "Here. I'll pass it over, and you hand it back under."

I reached for the rope with numb hands, moving now just by will, not because I wanted to move. The calf took a couple of kicks at me, swift cuts at my arm, but he missed. Tinker got the rope and tied it at the top of the calf's shoulders with a double knot. Then he bobbed his chin. "Climb up. I'll hold his head. Easy now, real easy."

I pulled myself up on the side of the chute and eased a leg onto the calf. He jerked, I pulled my leg back, then eased it over again, and still again. At last I was sitting on his back, feeling him quiver and heave beneath me, jamming my legs back and forth into the sides of the chute.

"You've got to be part of him," Tinker said in a whisper. "Let yourself down so you feel him."

I nodded, forcing my legs to relax, trying to settle. But it was no use, I couldn't get the right feel. That calf was farm, and I was city.

"Here, take the rope." He pushed the tail of the rope into my hand. "Wrap it around your wrist. That's how they do it at the rodeo—I saw it in a Gene Autry movie."

I didn't think. No part of my brain was working except the fear section, and it was pumping jolts down my back and into my eyes and throat. If I had been thinking I never would have wrapped the rope around my wrist, Gene Autry or not. By wrapping the rope, I became part of the calf—getting loose, at least in a hurry, became impossible. And I was beginning to have a feeling that I would want to get loose from the calf in a hurry.

But the rope was tight; Tinker helped me wrap it around my wrist not once or twice but a good four times, pulled tightly. I had my hand under it, squeezed against the calf's back.

"Are you ready?" Tinker asked.

I don't remember nodding but I must have, because Tinker moved around to the front and opened the chute.

I felt my teeth clench together as the calf saw freedom.

Parts of the ride didn't stay in my mind; they were driven out by the pounding and slamming. Power came from the calf's rear legs. After one or perhaps two great drives forward, I hung there, caught in the rope. I felt my stomach muscles heave with the pulling; then my neck jammed into itself when the calf's front end slammed into the ground.

The kids were screaming and yelling, and I think I was yelling too. For a couple of seconds, I had a flash of satisfaction because I was still on. Maybe it was the rope doing it, but I was still on, and by the third or fourth jump, I felt that I was learning about the calf. Something about the way he moved struck me, and I would lean into it. Where there had just been terror and the rope, now I felt that I was regaining balance and a little control. Even better, I could feel the calf slowing. He was tiring.

Then it happened. The rope around his front end had been tight when we left the chute, tight for the first few jumps. Now it seemed to loosen. Probably he had taken a breath in resistance when we pulled it tight. Now he let his breath out and made his rib cage smaller.

Whatever the reason, the rope became loose and started to slide to the right. Just a bit at first, then more and more as it became looser, and I was part of the rope, wrapped tightly in it.

I followed it. I went from the top of the calf down around his side with the rope, over and down as the calf ran in circles. Finally, I was underneath the calf. It was bad enough for him when I was on top. He had never

47

been ridden, and the sudden weight on his back had thrown him into a panic. Now it was worse. Now I hung beneath him, my flailing legs kicking up into his stomach, my head up between his front legs; a new and crazy attachment that he couldn't shake, couldn't jerk or pull away from, couldn't jump over.

He went wild. In spinning circles, he raced around the area in back of the barn, tearing through the muck and urine and manure as if his brain were on fire, pounding and driving to get me off.

I was under him, fighting to get out of the rope. But it took a long time. It took years. It took all the rest of my life to get the four wraps of rope from my wrist and detach myself from the insane animal.

When at last I had come loose and the calf was gone and I lay still in the manure, wondering if I was alive, I heard the laughter.

It was high and light and came from the children. I knew they were laughing at me, knew that it was because of the way I looked packed with mud and manure all over, and the hot worm came into my thoughts. The crazy thing came then, the awful thing. I stood and wiped my eyes and saw Tinker standing there in front of me laughing. I didn't care that I looked funny or that I had laughed at him or that he was nine and I was fourteen or that he hadn't meant to do it. All I saw was Tinker laughing and the rope burns around my wrist. All I could think of was that he had told me to take the rope, and I hit him.

I hit him in the face, on the nose, hit him hard, and

it was wrong. I hit him two or maybe three times, I don't remember, but there was blood from his nose going down through the freckles on his cheeks, blood that went down around the corners of his mouth and dripped in the dirt. His eyes grew wide with surprise and then hurt and fear, and I thought, *There, that will hold you for a while, you little puke.*

In the sudden silence after I hit him, I turned and walked around the barn. Later, shaking with hot tears of anger and frustration working down through the dirt on my face, I hated myself, hated what I had done and what I had been. But it was too late to be sorry, even though I was. Too late because David would have to know that I had gone back to being what I was in the city—something bad and without control, something terribly wrong.

6

‹‹‹‹‹‹‹‹‹‹‹‹‹‹‹‹‹‹‹‹‹‹‹‹‹‹‹‹‹‹‹‹‹‹ ‹‹‹‹‹‹‹‹‹‹‹‹‹‹‹‹‹‹

Nobody was in the kitchen except David and Emily. And of course me. David and I were sitting at the kitchen table. He had lighted his pipe, and I was staring at the shiny oilcloth tablecloth. There were scenes all over it, repeated every foot or so. There were pictures of little kitchens with little curtains and little stoves with little people cooking on them. I wished I were part of the world of the tablecloth. I wished I were anywhere but in the kitchen with David, who was quietly smoking his pipe and looking at the ceiling, watching a couple of miller moths circle the hissing lamp.

"So," he said after a time, a long time. "So, so, so . . ."

I didn't say anything. It had taken me a good half hour at the stock tank to get rid of most of the manure and mud. Some of it still stuck under my fingernails, and I made a great show of cleaning it out.

"It ain't right to hit when you're big and the other one is little. It ain't right to hit like that. Wrestling is one thing, but to hit that way . . ."

Emily turned from the stove. "It wasn't all wrong, David. Not straight out. They were riding calves, and he was dragged. I got it out of the kids after a bit of work. He was dragged through that muck in back of the barn, and they took to laughing at him. He got mad, that's all."

I looked up, surprised. Emily hadn't said ten words to me in two weeks and to have her taking my side caught me off guard.

"No," I said, turning back to David. "Even so, I shouldn't have hit Tinker. Even if I was mad. I just went kind of crazy or something because they were laughing at me. I'm sorry I did it, but it's done, and I can't make it go away."

And that surprised me, too. I hadn't planned on saying anything. Always before, when I got caught in trouble, I found that if I just kept my mouth shut and didn't admit to anything, it worked out for the best. Sometimes I had done things that I didn't even get blamed for. But this was different somehow. David wasn't like the police, or my mother, or the teachers. And Emily taking my

51

side, even after I'd hit her son—it all affected me and made me open my mouth.

David looked as surprised at my outburst as I felt. For another minute or two he said nothing, then he nodded. "It's not like we went into the stall blind, you coming up here to stay with us. Eunice told us you was coltish and that there had been trouble with you being wild and all. We knew that. Of course that don't make it right, you hittin' Tinker like that—we've got to do something about that."

Emily had gone back to the stove to take bread out, and the smell filled the kitchen. It is hard to think around the smell of fresh bread. All the other kids were upstairs, waiting to see what would happen. I knew the smell of the bread was going up the stairwell and that their mouths must be watering now.

"I could go home," I said. Somebody had to say it. The minute it was out, I knew that I didn't want to do it. Maybe I was only going to be here for the summer, or maybe longer into school—depending on the judge and my mother—but right then, no matter what I had done, I knew I didn't want to go back to the city. There was nothing there for me, not yet—it just felt wrong. Besides, if I went back, there was a good chance I would get sent to reform school. I had a friend named Jim Tison who went to reform school for what we did at the laundry one hot afternoon, standing in a tree and throwing rocks through the skylight. The broken glass cut one woman. I was released on probation because it was my first offense, but Jim had a long list of things he had done and they sent him to reform school. When he came back ten months later, he wasn't the same. The soft edges were out of his eyes, and his laughter cut. He told of things that I didn't believe at first, things about older boys and young men and the way it was to live in that place where they bought and sold and traded people.

I didn't want that. I didn't want any part of what Jim Tison had become and that's why I was afraid to say that I could go home.

"No. That won't work either." David scratched a match under the table, relighted his pipe, took some coffee. "That would be running from it. That ain't no way to fix anything, running. We got to fix this thing and make it work, and that means you've got to stay."

I breathed a little easier.

Emily faced us again. "He's too old to be playing. And there's nothing here in the line of work he knows how to do just yet. Besides we don't farm all that much that there's any work."

David turned to look at her. "Where you goin' with all this?"

"He could work at the smithy with you. He's old enough for that. And that would give him something to do for a time until he . . . changed."

I almost felt like I was eavesdropping. They were talking about me as if I weren't there. I started to say something, but David stopped me. "What do you think?"

I had a quick mental flash, remembering the stink of the blacksmith shop, the smoke from the horses hooves coiling up. "I'd like that," I said. "Maybe I could learn something." Which of course was what he wanted to hear. I knew it was, and that's why I said it. All the trouble I'd been in had taught me how to talk to grown-ups—you told them what they wanted to hear.

But this time I was wrong. I said what David wanted to hear, or so I thought, but I think now that he was onto me. He kind of smiled around his pipe and looked at the ceiling.

"Ya. Ya. Maybe it is you'll learn something," he said. "Maybe it is you'll learn more than you think, eh?" Then he stood and slapped his leg. "That's settled then. You come with me tomorrow. Now we go to bed."

I went upstairs and found my bunk in the dark and got into it and lay without sleeping for a time. Maybe it would all work out, but the picture of hitting Tinker, of the blood going down his cheek through the freckles, was still in my mind.

"Tinker," I whispered. "You awake?"

I didn't hear anything for a long time. I thought that either he was asleep or he didn't want to talk to me. I didn't blame him.

Then I heard a sigh in the dark. "Yeah. What do you want?"

"I'm . . ." I was going to say I was sorry, but it struck me that being sorry wasn't enough. "I was thinking about today. Riding that calf. What happened—I was just thinking about it."

"So?" His voice was tight, controlled. He was still mad.

"I must have looked pretty funny when I got thrown. I just wish I could have seen it from the side."

54

For a moment more there was silence, then I heard a kind of muffled grunting. I thought he was crying, and I felt bad. Then I realized he wasn't crying. He was laughing in his pillow, laughing until I could hear the springs in his cot squeak, laughing and pounding the side of the bed, laughing until I thought he would bust.

"You had—you had," he gasped, working to get it out. "You had cow crap underneath your *eyelids!* I've never seen anything like it. Everywhere you were brown, everywhere. It was packed in your ears—you had it all over. Just all over." And he burst out in a new wave of giggles.

I felt a smile coming—just a little tight smile—when I thought of how I must have looked. Then the smile widened as I remembered the helplessness of following the rope around the calf as the animal went over and down, like a dog on a leash, tearing at it to get it loose.

Pretty soon I was laughing with Tinker, and the night ended that way, with the two of us snorting into our pillows and the other kids picking it up and laughing and all of us feeding giggles to one another and making new laughter come until we finally drifted off to sleep.

7

<<<<<<<<<<<<<<<<<<<<<<<<<<<<<<<<<<<<<<<<<<<<<<<<<<

It never rained in the morning all the rest of that summer. It would often rain during the day, little dampers, but never in the morning when we were on the way into town with the team.

At first I had a feeling that I was being punished because of the trouble I had caused. But that wasn't it. David had just found a way to solve the problem so that it worked out for everybody. That was the way he lived.

"I'm not a blacksmith," he said the first morning as we drove the team to town. "That's only what people think I am because that's what they see me doing."

"But if that's what you do, isn't that what you are?"

He shook his head. "Nope. I'm a mechanic."

"I didn't know you worked on cars."

"I don't. I don't like them things. I said I was a mechanic, and a mechanic is somebody who fixes things. You show me something that's broke, or something that needs fixing or building, and I can do it. That's what a mechanic is, and that's what I am. But people call me a smith because I work at the smithy shop, and I just let them say it. But I'm really a mech—"

He stopped then because a small, long-legged bird had fluttered and dropped right ahead of the team and was scrabbling down the road dragging its left wing.

"Killdeer," he said, pointing with his chin. His hands were holding the reins back to slow the team. "See it?"

"It's got a broken wing," I said. "Look at it."

"Not this time. She's got chicks around somewhere. She's trying to pull us off so we won't find them. Look around. Look for cute little balls with stripes that are hidden under things."

He pulled the team up. I looked all up and down the side of the road from the wagon, but I couldn't see anything. By this time the mother was frantic, coming close to the horses and then turning and dragging her wings in the dirt and fluttering. When we didn't follow, she did it again and again. "I can't see them."

"Look harder. There's one by the right wheel of the wagon, just at the edge of the road. There. Under that piece of cardboard. See?"

And at last I did. A small bit of fluff with a tiny beak,

frozen under a small piece of cardboard at the side of the road. The chick had tiny stripes on the side and blended in so well with the dirt and grass that it was nearly impossible to make out.

"There'll be others around. Maybe six or seven. We'll let her fool us." He clucked twice down in his throat, and the team started forward slowly, as if afraid of stepping on the mother bird.

When we had moved down the road forty or fifty yards, with the mother flopping ahead of us all the way, she suddenly lifted off and flew around us and back to where she'd hidden the chicks.

"That was something—that was really something to see," I said, turning back to the front. "She really looked like her wing was broken."

"I've been running this team down this road to go to the shop for over ten years now. Wagon in the summer and sleigh in the winter. And I never get bored. There's always something to see. Always. Ain't it grand?" He spit in the dirt and looked up at the clouds. "It'll rain later. Summer rain. Crop rain. But not in the morning. Only in the spring and in the high fall just before snow does it rain in the morning. And speaking of rain reminds me of a marvel I ought to tell you about. Did you know that it sometimes rains hair snakes?"

I looked at him, and he went on to tell me about finding snakes made of long horsehairs swimming in rain barrels. I thought he was making it up. I thought he was just talking that first morning to keep my mind off the fact that I had to go with him, but he wasn't. I saw one of the snakes later. They are real.

I learned about David as the summer went on. He would tell me stories and I would think they were just made up. Then later I would find they weren't; they were real. Like once he told me about an old man in Norsten who could use a big, double-bladed ax to light a match. You put the match in a stump, head up, and he would swing the ax up and over and down and hit the match head to make it light. I didn't believe it. Then one day when I was working at the shop, cranking the bellows, an old man came in and sat down on the box of horseshoes in the corner.

"Nels," David said, looking up from the forge. "It's good to see you."

I was sure the man was Nels Thompson, although I had never met him.

David stood away from the forge, after pulling out a plowshare, and motioned me to come with him out back. "Nels, I wonder if you could light a match for this young man. I told him about you, and I don't think he believes me."

Nels got up and I followed, but I felt kind of bad because he was so old, so bent and worn and gray. His chest was sunken, his shoulders were sloped forward and down, and he sort of trundled when he walked. I was pretty sure he couldn't even lift an ax, let alone swing it, and I thought maybe David was playing some kind of a joke, even though he didn't do things like that. I didn't want the old man to feel bad.

As David went past the back door, he took an ax out of the woodbox by the side of the door. Then when he was in the back of the shop, he took a wooden match from his shirt pocket and jammed it down into a crack in the chopping block so the head stood straight in the air. All this time Nels was sort of doddering at the door, smiling in a vague way, and I was feeling worse because it seemed more and more like David was just playing a cruel joke. Nels hadn't said two words, and I even thought maybe his brain wasn't right. But I didn't know; I didn't know that Nels was from another time in the woods when an ax wasn't just a tool but a part of a man.

Nels came up to the chopping block and stood there, looking at the match, and I thought, *God this is awful,* but I didn't say anything. He just stood there, smiling, looking down at the block, waiting.

Then David put the ax on the ground next to Nels' feet, with the head down and the hickory handle propped against his old, bent leg. For a second, nothing happened. I think I started forward to take the ax and help Nels back into the shop.

But before I could move, Nels's hand sort of scrabbled around the side of his leg and fell across the hickory of the ax handle. What happened next was so strange I'm still not sure if it was real.

The axhead was down in the dirt. It looked too heavy for Nels to lift, but as I watched, it seemed to quiver. There was just a small shake of the steel in the dirt with little puffs of dust coming up around it. Then a shiver seemed to go up the wood and into his arm. I quit breathing. It was like the earth ran up the axhead and handle, through the steel and wood into the old man, and with that came power—you could see it go up the ax and into him. Not just power, but something more, too—maybe a kind of heat. Maybe it didn't all happen that way, but it seemed to. The power went up the ax and into his arm and into his body, and he moved straighter and stood taller and his shoulders came back. And then the ax rose, floated as if it were no more than a finger on his hand. It rose with his arm until it was high over his head, the sun flashing on the steel of the ax, catching light and flashing gold.

His other arm floated up and found the ax handle and for a second he stood there, poised, maybe younger than he'd ever been. I thought I had never seen anything so beautiful. When I looked over at David, I saw he was crying, and I realized I was crying, too.

Then the axhead came down, almost in slow motion, a great arc of gold steel, and the sharp front edge caught the head of the match. The steel gold of the ax mixed with the yellow gold of the fire as the match lit. My breath came out in an explosion.

"Thank you, Nels," David said. His voice was low and thick, and there were streaks down the grime of his cheeks from working over the forge. "I'd forgotten how that was—thank you."

I didn't trust myself to say anything, but later that morning when I went to the café and brought back coffee for the two men, I felt proud to be able to hand Nels a cup. He sat there for hours on the box of horseshoes, staring out the front door into the heat of the day, and every time I looked over at him, my throat would catch.

Watching Nels with the ax and the match was only

61

one of the things that made the summer full. Seeing the killdeer taking us away from the chicks was another. There were more, so many more, that all of the divisions of summer into early fall—which David called popcorn days and buttermilk nights—would help to fill the times in my life that were not so complete.

8

<<<<<<<<<<<<<<<<<<<<<<<<<<<<<<<<<<<<<<<<<<<<<<<<<

When I started working with David, we would get up
before daylight and help start the milking. Then when
all the cows were in and most of them milked, we would
harness the team and hook it to the wagon and start for
town and the smithy.

There was much that I would see and like without
understanding why I liked it: the smell of the cows, and
the sounds they made chewing their cuds, and the way
their eyes looked. The whole feel of the barn in the dark
of the morning when the light and mist off the fields first
came was beautiful. But more than that, it became a part

of my mind and maybe my soul, so that I found myself looking forward to it every morning. The thing is, for me to go from how I had lived in the city to looking forward to a barn full of cows every morning was quite a jump—and it just happened. The city part of my mind didn't understand it, and when I stood inside the barn taking in the smells and sounds, the new part of me couldn't believe that there ever had been a city with all the grays and alleys and hardness.

At first I thought working at the smithy was the biggest change, the biggest new thing. Maybe it was, only not in the way I thought.

I had seen David working on the horses, but other than that I had no idea what it was like to be a blacksmith. There were some pictures in my mind that had stuck somehow—pictures from schoolbooks—of burly men with leather aprons using big hammers against anvils. But that's not the way it was—or it was, but there was more, too. David wasn't burly, but what was there was awfully strong. Sometimes he didn't feel the pain from the hot steel until his skin was smoking—that's how thick his calluses had built up. He was always bent a little, from taking the weight of the horses when they leaned on him, but there was something big in him too, something you couldn't see but feel that made him a little like the blacksmiths in the schoolbooks.

But the school pictures that showed smithies all lighted up with the glow of fire were dead wrong. David's blacksmith shop was always gray and dark and smoky, and everything was covered with a layer of coal-smoke grease and black soot-dirt. And everything was heavy. Even plowshares—the removable bottom edge of the plow, the narrow edge that cuts the dirt—turned out to be heavy.

The first week David had me move a stack of boxes of old shares. They could be used again but only after being completely reshaped, and David needed them out of the way before the hard work began. But the boxes must have weighed over a hundred pounds each, so I had to take the shares out and move them one by one.

I became aware of the hardness and heaviness of steel when I first started working in the smithy with David. I didn't understand work, and I didn't understand how you made things work. Where I came from, if something broke, you either threw it away or bought a new part to fix it.

"We'll make do," David said again and again. "We'll make do with old iron and fire."

And he would take some old scrap and make a whole new part, working it on the anvil with a hammer or over on the trip-hammer.

In fact, most of the work I did in the shop was to turn cranks. One big handle turned the bellows pump to bring the fire to new heat. Another crank was on the back of the big steel flywheel that ran the "automatic" trip-hammer. Without electricity to run a motor, the trip-hammer had to be run by hand.

"Mr. Hammer," David would say. "Turn me up, Mr. Hammer." And I would start the big flywheel round and round to bring the steel top hammer slamming down on the bottom square anvil, just like a big jaw or nutcracker. *Poom POOM, poom POOM,* it rang, hammering down in a rhythm like a great steel drum as David worked the piece of steel he was making around and back and forth.

Sparks showered on him, caught in his cuffs, and sometimes smoldered. At first I hated that flywheel handle. Every morning we came in and fired up the forge and started heating steel and then started the trip-hammer. The only break we got was shoeing horses, but that didn't happen often. Although I hated the wheel at first, that soon changed. The wheel became a part of me, or maybe I became a part of the trip-hammer wheel: It became *my* part of the smithy. A place for me to be.

So I was the wheel, I was Mr. Hammer, and many things I used to think were important no longer were. I came to look for good steel, steel that made a rich blue color as it got hot, as David taught me. And I forgot about life back in the city. There was nothing for me back there—nothing to remember.

Or almost nothing. One morning we were going to town and David spit over the side of the wagon and looked at the horses for a minute, searching for something I couldn't see, and then he looked at me. "In the city down there, in Minneapolis—what's it like to live there?"

"How do you mean?"

"Eunice, your mother, my sister, she came from this country, and she went down there to work in a plant and married your father. There ain't nobody up here who knows what it's like to live down there. I thought maybe you could tell me."

I looked out over the horses, and I couldn't think of anything right away that David would be able to understand. Then it hit me. "You know how the last couple of nights we went out and looked at the sky?"

"Ya. Ya. It was pretty, wasn't it?"

It had been beautiful. Stars just splattered all over and the sky so bright and open and free that it didn't seem real. "In the city, you never see the sky at night."

"No."

"That's the truth. There's so much light from the streetlights and signs and things like that the stars don't get through."

For half a mile we rode in silence, and then he turned to me. "That must be a heavy load to handle, ain't it?"

I didn't say anything. I was thinking of other things I could tell him. Now that I had started, they were coming in a flood. "There's noise all the time. It's never quiet. Cars and sirens and just a kind of hum so you never hear birds but just the sound of the city going all the time."

"Ya. Ya. I figured that. But what I meant was, what are the people like?"

"Oh." Again I spent some time thinking. "Well. I guess they're just people, like everywhere else." And of course I knew that wasn't the truth, but I had run into a corner because I started thinking about David and the blacksmith shop against the city. He just wouldn't understand. To most of the people I knew in Minneapolis, David would be considered a kind of jack-pine savage. And if I told him how I had truly lived, shooting nineball and standing on the sides of the street and looking smooth, none of it would make sense to him. It would all just seem stupid.

And that's what was happening in my own mind as

well. When I used the city part of my brain, it seemed crazy to be doing what I was—working with an old farmer in a blacksmith shop, riding a wagon every morning behind a team of horses, sleeping in a room with seven other people, getting up before daylight, washing in a stock tank, and working all day in the stink and heat of the forge.

But I was changing and sometimes, as the summer moved through its stages, I would stop what I was doing or think while I was working and I couldn't believe that I once just stood on the corner making wise-snot comments to passing people.

I don't know when the change started. It seems like halfway through the summer or so, one midmorning I turned from the bellows and grabbed a horseshoe to hand to David. Suddenly I saw myself as I had been and as I was becoming.

Just in physical appearance, the changes were striking. In the city I had worn jeans and T-shirts and been more or less careless about how I dressed. But I was soft white, like my friends. Maybe I looked good, or at any rate looked like the rest of them, but it was all on the surface. I was thinnish then, of medium height and stood with a slight slouch, and I was pale all the time.

Now I could have looked in a mirror and not known myself. I stood taller, straighter, because I had been lifting things that had weight—horses' legs, plows, steel, and iron. My arms and legs and chest had filled out for the same reason. No fat, just hard muscle, and I was tanned smoke-brown from working without a shirt in the summer, working over the forge and then going out in the sun. My face was almost black from it, except where I wore a leather strap around my forehead to keep the sweat from dripping down into my eyes. My hair had been a brown-blond in the city and it was now flash-white when I washed it. The day finally came when David looked at me and said, "You ain't the same."

I shook my head and maybe I spit. "No. I'm not."

It was true. I was different inside, too, different from anything I had been. There was a new feeling in me—not just a change but a whole new thing. I thought differently. I didn't think everybody was against me anymore—I didn't feel that the whole world had been designed just to dump garbage on *my* head, which I had come to believe for a time in the city. I was still fourteen, still caught in the same world, but there was something else now. I was . . . settled, somehow. I saw and knew things I hadn't seen and known before.

One day a girl named Jenny—Jennifer—came by the smithy with some tools her father wanted heat-treated. She was carrying them in a basket. She was about my age and had long blonde hair and blue eyes that lifted at the corners. She walked like a deer I had seen on the way to town one morning, and she had a voice like a song. I saw all that when I looked at her, saw what I wouldn't have seen before, when I would have made some jackass comment or other and never have known her at all.

As it turned out, I walked some of the summer evenings with Jenny and watched her brush the hair out of her face and listened to her tell me her dreams. Later, when I saw the inside of David and wanted to understand him, I talked to Jenny about it and she helped me. Maybe later I shone for Jenny and maybe still later I came to love Jenny, because of my changing and because of the joy of David and the circus. None of it, none of it would have happened if I hadn't come north and gone to work at the smithy with David.

Toward the end of summer, I thought about Jim Tison. I had just finished firing the forge to get it ready for work—making a wood fire and then adding slow-burning coal until there was a bed for the steel—and I went to the water barrel by the door for a drink from the dipper. The water was still cold, and what I didn't drink I poured over my head. I looked out into the street and the dust, and I thought of Jim Tison and the expression in his eyes when he came back from reform school. It was a clean, uncluttered thought—just a straight line.

If Jim Tison had had this to come to, I thought, *he never would have been ruined.* And with the thought came a sadness for Jim. I felt that maybe when I went back, *if* I went back to the city, I would tell him of what I had found and how I had changed.

But then it was the time of high summer, and my life was so full that I didn't think again of Jim Tison.

70

9

<<<<<<<<<<<<<<<<<<<<<<<<<<<<<<<<<<<<<<<<<<<<<<<

"Maybe nothing just happens suddenly," David said. "It's like steel when you hammer to weld it. You get it hot, then hotter, until it all just flows together. Then it's right. Maybe everything is like that."

He had been working on broken equipment all morning. In the spring, people wanted their horses shoed and the plowshares hammered out into sharp edges. In between low summer and high summer, they wanted wagons made or wheels fixed, and in high summer with the harvest approaching, they wanted their equipment repaired. There were mowers for cutting hay, swatters for cutting ripe grain and laying it in windrows to be picked up by the shaulker—which made it into shaulks to be carried to the threshing machine—grain wagons to haul the grain, and horses' hooves. All of this was old, or getting old, and would break down and need fixing.

As the smell of coming harvest took over, the town settled into a kind of never-rest feeling that spread to the smithy also. I thought I had learned about work earlier that summer, and many nights I fell asleep on the wagon going home, leaning against David while the slow movement of the team closed my eyes and my mind.

But now the work took on a whole new meaning. We left before daylight, left in hard dark as Emily and the children took over the milking. The forge would still be hot from the day or night before. When we got home after work late at night, after eating a couple of mouthfuls of food, I would fall into bed, sometimes without even taking my clothes off.

It wasn't a bad tired feeling, though. It was a full tired feeling. I never seemed to get short-tempered about the work even though there was no money. Some of the time I was numb, but once or twice I even thought it was nice to be working like that.

One noon I looked out the smithy door down the dusty road leading to the depot, and there were wagons and farm implements lined up waiting to be repaired. The line was a quarter of a mile long, maybe a little more, of equipment people had pulled in and just left, trusting that we would be able to get to it. To be trusted that way, to just work and work and be part of the line of equipment, to be trusted—there was beauty in that.

That same day Jenny came down to the smithy with lunch for me in a half-gallon metal lard pail. Sometimes we had lunch at the café, where we would sit and listen to the farmers talk if they happened to be in town. But this one day, for no reason, Jenny brought me lunch in a pail. I opened the lid to find cold chicken and fresh bread dripping with honey wrapped in a small check-ered towel. There was also a pint jar of water-chilled fresh milk. I sat on the bench in front of the smithy and ate and drank everything, piece by piece, swallow by swallow, chewing slowly and tasting it all and letting the food work down my throat easily. It tasted so good my jaws ached, and I didn't say anything. Jenny laughed.

"What's the matter?" I asked.

"You're so quiet. Just sitting and chewing like that, staring down the street—you make me think of a serious old man."

She knew all about me and, of course, how old I was—she was the same age—because when we walked in the evenings, we often talked about what we wanted. Jenny moved as softly as the summer nights and we would hold hands and it was gentle. Sometimes we walked for an hour without saying anything. It wasn't necessary to speak.

I had never acted what you'd call serious or older than I was, and I didn't mean to act that way now. "I was just thinking that all these people really need David, and David really needs all these people." I nodded up the street at the lineup of farm implements.

"Yes. It works both ways."

I chewed a piece of chicken and swallowed, still looking down the street. "I've never seen that before. Not like this. I never thought anybody needed anybody else. Where I lived, it worked the other way. If you needed somebody you were weak, and it was weakness when other people needed you."

"This way is better."

"Yes. It is. I'm glad I'm here."

"I'm glad you are, too."

David had come back then, and we had pulled in a John Deere horse-drawn mower and gone back to work. But Jenny had left a warm place in me, and not just from the good food. The rest of that afternoon went by easily into evening.

It was probably during that afternoon that David first got the idea for the circus, although he never said so.

We had to put new bearings in the mower and take the sickle bar out to sharpen the teeth on the triangular-shaped grinder in the back of the smithy. It wasn't hard, but there was a lot of machinery to take apart and put back together. I held the wrenches for David as he worked. He swore lightly now and then to make a bolt go in right or come out easier.

"Machines is all right if they do what you want them to do," he said when the mower was done and we'd pulled it outside. People would bring the equipment in with their teams and then take the teams off to pasture or back home if we couldn't get the implement fixed right away. We would just pull them out of the building by hand when they were fixed, and the owners would come to pick them up with the teams again. That way the horses didn't have to stand around and draw flies and heat if there was a long wait.

When the mower was out to the side, we dragged another mower in. I started removing the sickle bar while David worked at the head of the sickle housing to pull the bearing out and put a new one in.

"You take a mower," he continued, grease to his elbows. "You want to cut hay, you can't beat a mower. But it won't spread manure worth a tinker's snot-rag."

I smiled and nodded.

"A mechanic, now, or a smithy—*there's* the fellow who makes the machine do what it's supposed to do. That's what I meant by everything flowing together and not coming sudden. You see what I mean?"

I didn't, but I didn't say anything. I could ask him or not ask him, it didn't make any difference. He'd get to it and tell me sooner or later anyway.

"Take a fellow out there, he wants to cut some hay to feed his stock through the winter and his mower is broke. We've got to fix it. Then later when the stock leaves manure and he wants to spread it and his manure spreader is broke, we've got to fix that, too. It all takes time, and it all flows together."

Again I nodded, but I didn't see what he was getting at until two nights later when we quit just a bit early—nine o'clock—and went home.

It was a Saturday night, and the whole family had to

take baths. That meant heating water in the boiler on the wood stove and taking sit-down baths in the tub on the porch. The kids took theirs during the day, or late afternoon, and David and I took ours out in the dark while Emily heated and brought water and made us plates of meat and potatoes.

We bathed and ate and sat for a little time at the table before going to bed. It was late, and the kids were already upstairs asleep, but with the high-summer rush on this was the only time David and Emily got to talk. I still had some pie and milk to finish, so I happened to hear them talking.

Emily was at the stove and David was sitting at the table, smoking a pipe and drinking coffee.

"There's a circus coming down to Halton," Emily said. "There's a lot of talk of it."

I'd heard some of the talk. Halton was a medium-size town about forty miles south. It could have been in another state as far as most of the people in Norsten were concerned. Forty miles was considered a vast distance. I had been to circuses, of course, in the city. We used to sneak in all the time, and get thrown out by the roustabouts. But a circus coming this far north, to these small towns, was considered big stuff. It didn't happen that often.

"I know about the circus." There was a note in David's voice I'd never heard before, something tight and hard. "I don't see that it concerns us."

"John Claypool is getting together a bunch of people to go down to Halton to see it." Emily continued as if

David hadn't spoken. "Taking the school bus. All the kids is talking about it."

David put his pipe down and pushed his cup around a little on the table, looking at the oilcloth. "I don't see how it can be free."

"It ain't free," she said. "It's a dollar a kid to go down there, and then they need another dollar to get in."

"That'd be . . ."

"Right at sixteen dollars," Emily finished for him.

"You had that figured fast."

"I had it figured before."

"Sixteen dollars is a lot of money," he said, looking up. And now I could feel what it was in his voice. It was sadness. "We don't have it."

"I know," she said. "I knew that when I first figured it out. I looked in the jar when I first figured it out, and we've got twelve dollars. And we can't spend all of the money we have on a circus."

David said nothing.

"It's just that kids should have at least one circus to look back on later when they need to."

I was going to say something then. I was going to say that I had been to plenty of circuses and that they weren't much. It all looked good at first, but when you saw it close there were tears in the costumes and old drunks who helped set up the tents. I was going to say that circuses weren't worth all the bother, but I didn't. It wasn't the time to speak.

David was staring down at his hands. They were dirty and scarred and huge, but now they looked kind of helpless. Or maybe the helplessness was in his eyes.

"What is it when a man hasn't got money to send his kids to one circus?" he asked. He didn't expect an answer, and neither Emily nor I said anything. "There just ain't the money for it—but what can it be when a man hasn't got sixteen dollars for his kids?"

I was done with my pie, and if I hadn't been done, I wouldn't have been able to eat it anyway. He was always so happy, so ready. Now he just sat. At first I was mad at Emily for making him that way, but then I knew it wasn't her fault. I stood up and made for the stairwell door, but just at the door I turned and looked back at David sitting at the table.

"If I had the money," I said, and my voice was low and choked a little. "I'd, well, give it to you."

But he didn't turn and just sat looking down at his hands. I went up to bed but didn't sleep for a long time, even though I was so tired my muscles burned.

10

<<<<<<<<<<<<<<<<<<<<<<<<<<<<<<<<<<<<<<<<<<<<<<<<<<<

For a week after that talk at the stove, work piled up on us. There was a new feeling in the air, more and more urgent. The grain in the fields was getting ripe and ready to cut. It was the kind of thing that didn't allow for any loose time. When the grain got ripe, it had to be cut. Period. Cut in long golden rows to dry and be made into shaulks and picked up so the grain could be threshed out and sold. Or bartered because there was no money. And once all of that started it didn't matter if you were tired or young or old or upside-down or eating cake—all that mattered was the grain. It had to be harvested before it spoiled.

The whole town felt it. Stores stayed open later, and people were on call if they were needed. At the blacksmith shop, we just slept on cots at the back and ate and worked and slept and worked until it was impossible to tell one time from the next. The line of equipment would get shorter or longer, it didn't seem to matter. Usually women, since the men were working in the fields, would bring in broken, shattered, or crumbled pieces of wheels or gears or cutters or wagons, and they all had to be fixed immediately.

The forge never went out, never cooled. I spent most of my time at the handle of the bellows, keeping it at a high whine while various pieces of steel got hot and David stayed on the hammer, tap-*tap*ing in sparks and heat and fire until something was fixed or something new was shaped. Then on to the next piece.

We worked until we began dropping things. Then we would sleep for an hour or a little more or less and again we were up. I would crank the whine into life, and David would pick up his hammer or tongs. I thought it would never end.

Jenny brought food for us. And sometimes Emily came into town and brought more food, which we ate with our fingers. David drank coffee from a quart jar wrapped in newspaper to keep it hot, and I drank milk in another jar wrapped to keep it cold. We had chicken and pork chops and venison steak and whole potatoes, and it all tasted of the high dry spit of burning coal and steel.

More than once, I did not think I could take it anymore. More than once, a moment would come during the week when I would stop and start to cry, not with sadness or anger but with a kind of rage that there could be only me and the bellows and the flame and the steel. Then David would look over at me and smile through his black-burned face, and I would answer the smile and keep going.

Nothing was left of my old life. Nothing of the trouble I had been in, nothing of the fights with my mother or the bad things I had done or the breaking of things—none of that existed anymore. Only the work.

And then it was done.

A week, a month, a year, a lifetime had gone by. One day I went to the doorway, staggering, and looked down the street, and there was no next broken machine. Just the empty street. I went to the big table by the door to get the next broken piece, and there wasn't one.

"There's nothing," I said. "There's nothing next."

David stood away from the anvil slowly, put his hammer down like he was laying down his arm. He smiled. "That's the way of it. Just when you hit your stride, they quit on you."

"Hit your stride . . ." I hurt all over. It just couldn't be over, I thought—it was going to last forever. I was numb. "Some stride."

But he wasn't listening. He had walked to the door and looked up and down the street, one hand up on the edge of the big door opening, standing bent and tired, but relaxed somehow. It looked like a painting, him standing in the door, slouched over with his leather apron burned black and his hair smoked into tight gray-black curls and the smoke of steel all over him.

"What day is it?" he asked without turning. "Is it Friday?"

I had to think for a minute. Days had gone into nights and back into days and more days and nights until there was just a blend of time. "No. I think it's Saturday. Or is it Sunday? No. It's Saturday."

He said nothing for a moment, then turned away from the door opening. His shoulders were just a bit sagged, and he was as dirty as me, dirty down to the inside of his skin, the dirt so deep it was part of him.

"It's Saturday? Are you sure?"

"Yes. No. Yes. I know it is because the milk truck went through, and they only go through this way on Saturday. Why? Does it make all that much difference?"

He spit. "Ya. It makes a little difference. I'm going to get roaring drunk, and I'd hate to drink when it wasn't a Saturday night. I would have done it anyway, but I hate to. It's good that it's Saturday." He took off his apron and carefully hung it on a nail by the horse stall and walked out into the late afternoon sun.

For a moment, I thought I'd follow him and make sure he was all right. But then I went to the back of the shop and fell on the cot. I was asleep before my head hit the little gray pillow.

After that wild week I was past sleep, past the normal depth and movements of sleep. My head mashed down into the bed, my shoulders ground into the thin mattress,

82

and I don't know how long I would have stayed that way if someone hadn't started jerking me back and forth and pulling my head around.

I awakened slowly. Parts of me were sticky and thick. When I finally got my eyes open, I saw Jenny in the darkness.

"Wake up. Wake up now!" Her hand on my shoulder pulled me over, and I sat up. My whole body ached, deep ache, hard ache, and there was forge and coal-stink taste caked in my mouth.

"What's the matter?" I fought sleep away, stood and made my way to the tempering barrel. There was water there for cooling and hardening steel, and I splashed some of it on my face. A little went into my mouth, and I spit the forge taste out. "What time is it?"

"It's eleven o'clock. My dad sent me down here to get you."

"Your dad? Why?"

"It's David. He needs you."

"What are you talking about?"

"Come on. Now."

She turned and made for the door, and I stumbled after her, still not fully awake. Out in the street, the moon was full, and Jenny turned and made for the center of town, where the café and beer hall were. All lights were out except those from the beer hall. When we got there, she went right in even though you weren't supposed to go in unless you were over twenty-one.

By this time, I had more or less figured out what was happening. I had seen drinking before, lived surrounded

83

by bars and winos. When you are needed to help with someone at eleven at night, it doesn't take a genius to come up with some answers.

But I was wrong.

Inside the bar, there were four or five men sitting at the card tables in the rear. They were old and came to play cards. They didn't drink, but they more or less lived in the bar. On their small government checks, they couldn't afford to do much else, and there was always a table kept open for these old men to sit and play a card game called smear. The bartender was also an old man, and he was behind the rough wood bar. Over the bar a Coleman-type lantern was hissing white light, and in the light stood David. His elbows were propped on the wood, and there was a bottle of beer in front of him. He was staring down at his hands just the way he had done in the kitchen that night a week ago.

Next to David, but a foot or two away, stood another man about his age whom I recognized as Jenny's father. He was a woodcutter and didn't have work to do in the summer other than getting ready to cut in the fall and winter. He was a good friend of David's and must have been called down to help.

When I walked up to the bar, I saw that David was very, very drunk. His eyes would blink only slowly, as if he had to work at it, and when I stopped next to him, it took several seconds for him to turn his head and focus on me.

"Boy," he said. "You . . . here? Why's 'at? Why aren't you at the circus?"

I said nothing. Across from him, Jenny's father caught my eye. "Help me get him to the smithy."

He took one arm and I took the other and we shoved and carried David out of the saloon. It took us a full twenty minutes to get him down the street to the shop and in the back, where he fell on a cot and—I thought—went to sleep.

"He keeps talking about that circus," Jenny's father said. "You know why?"

"No." I shook my head. "He's just tired and drunk. It's been a lot of hard work."

"I know. Well, good night."

Jenny gave me a private look, and they left. I moved back to my cot and sat on the edge and wondered if I could harness the team and take David home. Then I thought better of it and decided to let him sleep it off. The hard work was done, and the next day we could quit early and go home and take baths and eat. Everything would be all right.

I fell back on the blanket and closed my eyes. I would have slept except that David sat up.

"What is it," he mumbled, "when a man can't take his kids to the circus?"

"I think you should try to go to sleep," I said. "We'll talk about it tomorrow."

"No," he said, and I realized that he was sitting there crying. "No. We won't talk about it tomorrow. Talking never did anything about getting anything done. That's what's wrong now—everybody talks. No. I'm through talking."

For a few seconds there was silence and I thought he had lain back down in the darkness, but he was still up. I finally said, "What are you going to do?"

"I'm going to take my kids to the circus," he said, suddenly laughing. "And you can come too."

"But it costs too much."

"Ya. That's for sure. That's why we're going to do it here. Right here in Norsten."

I thought he had just gone crazy with the drink. I had seen lots of winos in the city go mad with drinking. They would see spiders or talk about friends whom they saw, but who weren't there. Their faces would get red, and they would die with the madness of drinking. I was afraid that David was going the same way. "They'll never bring the circus to Norsten," I said, trying now to keep him talking until he made sense.

"Ya. Ya. I know that," he said. "To hell with them. I'm going to make my own."

"Make your own what?"

"I'm going to make my own circus. I'll start tomorrow."

And then he fell back. This time he slept, and I did the same.

Tomorrow, I thought, going under to the quiet rasp of his breathing. *Tomorrow we'll go home. Emily will cook a meal, and he will be normal again. Tomorrow it will be all right. . . .*

11

<<<<<<<<<<<<<<<<<<<<<<<<<<<<<<<<<<<<<<<<<<<<<<<<<

The ringing of steel awakened me. I was stiff and sore and not ready to come awake yet. When I heard the hammer, I thought I was dreaming. Then, when I came fully awake, I thought maybe nothing had changed and we were still working with the harvest panic on us.

But finally I opened my eyes and put my feet on the floor, and there was David at the anvil, working in the dawn light that came through the door. There was smoke moving across him from the forge. He had a long piece of strap iron, ten or twelve feet, and he was shaping one end around, kissing it with little taps of the hammer

87

while I went to the tempering barrel and threw water on my head.

"Something break down?" I had not forgotten last night and the talk we'd had, but I was hoping he had. He had been drunk, deep drunk, and I figured it was a good bet that most of what he had said was gone in the fuzz.

"No."

"What is it, then?" Of course I didn't know all the parts of the implements after only one summer working at the smithy, but I knew some, and I didn't recognize this piece of iron.

He gave the iron two more taps and stuck it back in the bed of coals to reheat. With a slight nod, he motioned me to the bellows and I started working the crank. Sometimes he would do that, not answer me—especially when he was thinking about what he was working on—but this time he was just thinking about what to say to me. He filled his pipe and lit it, blowing smoke, and then he reinspected the iron. It was still only getting red, not white, and he didn't like it yet.

"I'm building a circus," he said. It came out fast, quick on the edges, but it wasn't sad or down. "I told you last night."

"Yeah. But you . . . I mean I wasn't sure what you meant then."

"I meant what I said—I'm going to build a circus for my kids. And I want you to help me because you're my assistant." Drag, smoke. "And because I need help."

I stared down into the fire. A quick picture came into

my mind of David gone crazy and wild and his brain wasted, but I pushed it away. "Sure. I'll help. But I still don't understand. How are you going to build a circus?"

"We'll build it from the graveyard," he said. "Out of steel and old parts."

I nodded, although he still wasn't making any sense to me. The graveyard was a field out to the side of the smithy where all the old broken machinery was left. Someday it would be called a junkyard, but then it was the graveyard. But that didn't help me. A circus was clowns and animals and sideshows and rides. "I'm still a little confused," I admitted.

"Sure, sure. But look now, look here." He left the forge, and I dropped the bellows crank and followed to the dirt in the middle of the floor, where he knelt and took a sharp stick.

"When you don't have money, you have to make what you need. I forgot that for a while last night." He smiled up at me. "That's why I got so drunk. Then I remembered. Look here now."

The stick started to move and draw pictures in the dirt, which at first didn't make any more sense to me than how he had been talking.

A line here and a circle there—even after a summer of working with him and watching him make drawings in the dirt for the farmers, I was lost for a time. Then a shape came, a curve met another curve and there, in the dirt on the floor of the smithy, was a merry-go-round. It didn't have horses, but it had seats, and there was a motor in the middle. It was big, you could tell that from the size of the kids he drew to sit on it. I was sure he was crazy. *You can't just make a merry-go-round,* I thought. *You can't just* make *one.*

Then he used a hand to wipe everything away. He looked up. "And see. More. See now."

And the stick started to move again, deft little strokes, and a Ferris wheel grew in the dirt. Not as huge as the merry-go-round, but large even so, with another kind of motor in the middle. Finally, he erased that and drew another ride of some kind, but by then it didn't matter because I wasn't really looking anymore. I was wondering how I could get word to Emily that he had gone crazy, get word that we had to get him home.

I nodded. "All right. All right. I'll help." And all the time I was thinking that I'd just go along with him until I could get help. Sometimes Emily came in during the day to talk with him, or one of the kids would ride in on a pony or even walk in. Maybe I could keep him from hurting himself until then.

Before he was done, he had gone all around the floor of the smithy in the dirt, drawing pictures. Most of them didn't make any sense to me except that they were obviously machinery, and he meant them to be a circus.

When he had finished, he stood in the middle, grinning around the dirt in his face, grinning around the hangover. "See? Do you see how it goes?"

I didn't then, but again I nodded.

"All right. You start on the bellows then. You start now, by God, and we'll do her."

I moved to the forge and added coal and built a small

wood fire over the top of it and started cranking the bellows when it was going well. Soon the flame went hot red and then white. When the coal fired and went white, David took the long piece of iron he'd been working on and pushed it down into the coal.

He looked up at me and smiled. I smiled back, but I don't think I've ever felt so sad. I thought he was broken, broken-down just like the machines we had been working on so hard, and I wondered if there was a way I could fix him.

Parts of what happened next, over the following week and a half, don't seem real—they were real, but they couldn't be, and so they don't come through memory in a clear way. It's more like paintings mixed with music so that the memory doesn't flow but is frozen into pictures.

David started as a smithy who was working to build something he needed—a circus for his kids. And I started as a helper. But then everything changed.

I thought we had worked hard before—I didn't know what work was, had no idea. The heat from the forge cooked my face into blisters, peeled the blisters, and then recooked it into more blisters. The process repeated itself until I was leather, until my skin matched my leather sweatband. I was coal, I was fire, I was heat and movement and the *crang CRANG* of hammer to metal and the shower of sparks—I was all of these things just in the first two days and I became a deeper part of them in the following days.

David became steel and smoke and the hammer. When I think of him now, I see him as a flash of white teeth smiling through the burned black of his face and the shower of sparks and the hammer raising and coming down and the steel bending.

I know we ate. I know people brought us food, but I don't remember one meal. Jenny came many times with food, but I can't think of one piece of food that I ate. It was just something that we had to do.

Emily came and went. She took me aside. I was going to tell her I was worried about David because of what he was doing, but I didn't. Something had happened between us, something made of fire and steel, and if David was crazy by then, so was I.

"He gets like this sometimes," she said, smiling at me. "I used to worry, but I don't anymore. It's too grand for worry. But I'm concerned about you. Are you all right?" She was looking at my face with real care in her eyes.

I felt warm to think that she really cared, but I shook my head. "There's nothing to worry about. I'm fine. I'm fine." I just wanted to get back to the forge, get back to my bellows and the steel and fire. "I have to go. The forge is cooling, the steel is cooling. I have to go." And I turned and left her, and she went home.

The merry-go-round was first. Out in back of the smithy, north of the graveyard for broken machinery, there was a forty-acre field that was left fallow. It was grown over with short grass because sometimes the farmers tethered their teams there when they came to town and the horses had cropped it down.

In the middle of the field, David had me dig a hole

with the large posthole digger. He sank an iron pipe into the ground in base gravel, and we packed dirt around it to make it stout and hard.

This was the center of the merry-go-round, the core on which it was to be built. Then David took old iron wagon wheels and welded them into place on the pipe top and bottom, for drivers with prefit iron brackets, and when the wheels were in place, he fit a pulley to the middle as well. Then he went back into the smithy, and we fired up the forge. He made iron rods and iron straps that crossed over them to keep them stiff. We put the rods in place by bolting them to the wheels. Then we bolted the iron straps to the rods and to each other until there was one giant wheel with six spokes sticking out about twenty feet.

Out in the graveyard, he took seats from old swatters and mowers, iron seats with holes in the bottom, old tractor seats. He fashioned more brackets and put six of the seats into position on the end of the spokes so they were hanging down a little. Then, in front of each seat, he bolted a bracket to hold on to. Finally he worked a motor with a belt drive into the middle and bolted it to the center shaft. When he was done, he found a can of red paint and a brush, which he handed to me with a smile. "Now you paint, and I'll start on the next one."

"But aren't you going to test the motor on it, see if it works?" I asked, holding the paint and brush.

"For what? I fixed the motor, it will work. Now get to it. I need you back on the forge as soon as you're finished."

So I painted, and when the merry-go-round was all

bright and shiny red in the sun, I pushed it once. It turned easily, and I started then to think that even if David couldn't make a circus, one thing was sure: He was going to give it one mighty push of a try.

I went back to the smithy with the merry-go-round still wheeling in the late summer sun.

12

<<<<<<<<<<<<<<<<<<<<<<<<<<<<<<<<<<<<<<<<<<<<<<<<<

The change came over David about the same time the
change came over the town. I don't remember which day
it was, but I saw it in David first.

His face was lighted somehow. We were working on
the Ferris wheel arms—the Ferris wheel would have
four arms and four seats that went up and over. We were
at the forge heating the metal to bend it around to fit into
the seats when I saw his face.

It took me a minute to figure out the expression. I
thought he was flushed from the heat of the forge, but
that wouldn't be new because we'd been working hard

at the forge for weeks now. Then I thought maybe he
had gotten into the beer again or was sneaking it somehow, but that was impossible.

I finally realized that he was just completely, totally,
deeply happy.

"You . . . you look different," I said, over the smoke
from the forge. "You don't look at all the same."

"I am the same. Only better." He laughed, long and
deep. "Ya. I'm a better same now."

And we went back to the flow of work. Steel went
from red to white, was shaped, then drilled on the big
crank drill press, and bolted to more steel. Finally, in
back, on two large steel posts sunk in gravel, there rose
the skeleton of a Ferris wheel, all shaped out of old scraps
and wheels and belts from the graveyard.

It took us a full day just to get the four skeleton arms
up. The work was hard, and it was getting dark. I was
becoming more than a little sick of it all when I noticed
that we weren't alone.

Wilton Moen, who worked at the depot, was standing
next to me as I helped to lift a spoke up, and he reached
up beside me.

"Here. Let me help, then."

He held it while I put a bolt through a hole and tight-
ened it down with a wrench. Then he turned to help
David get the next arm in position, and we had all the
arms in place before dark. You could tell what it was
going to be. I stood for a minute and stared up at it
against the night-coming sky, and I thought how won-
derful it was that a man could start with nothing but an
idea and make a circus from old scrap.

David had gone back to the shop to start on the next part, the seats. But Wilton stayed with me for a moment.

"I was down to the state fair in Minneapolis one time," he said, smiling up at the Ferris wheel frame against the sky. "And it was something to see, but it didn't hold nothing to this. More'n once David has taken the town by surprise. But this . . . this . . . I just had to help."

In the morning when I washed my face in the rain barrel and turned to the forge, I saw more people standing in the door to the smithy. Jenny was there with rolls and milk, and to each side of her there were men and women. I knew some of them, but some I hadn't seen before. They all had on work clothes. A few people were wearing gloves, and others had jars of coffee with paper wrapped around them.

David nodded to them as if he had expected to see them. There was nothing said, no instructions issued of any kind, yet everybody went to work and seemed to know just what to do. And when that day was losing light and turning to dark, the Ferris wheel stood, painted yellow with red seats and powered by an old Fairbanks Morse pump engine with a flywheel. It rolled against the sky, but nobody had ridden it yet.

More people had come and they were working on anything that needed doing, from bringing food to painting. Now and then, they even spelled me on the forge, and by midnight we had made a dent in finishing up another ride with swings that went around in a circle. Nobody went home.

There was the smell of sweat now with the smell of smoke and iron from the forge, and we slept in little corners—I dozed sitting by the forge with my head on Jenny's shoulder. When it was time to work again, somebody brought coffee and milk and more rolls and sandwiches, and we ate and went to work. The next day we finished the circus.

Emily and the kids came in about midday. They were dressed for work, and they pitched in with everybody else. The swing seat ride was done. Then people started making booths from wood they brought and stretched colored cloth across them. Somebody brought some ponies for rides, and by late afternoon the circus was done. All done.

Everybody stood in silence, looking at what they had done. What *we* had done. Where there had been a ragged old field of chewed-down pasture grass, there was a circus. Or maybe it could be called a fair. There were booths and rides and color splashing in the sun.

David had made a circus. While we all stood at one end, he went into it, walking in the area between the rides and the booths. He walked all the way down and all the way back, and I heard somebody next to me whisper, "Look, David's got the shine on him. *Look* at it."

And there was something about him that shone. There was light about him, strength and joy in him. He turned, shook his head, and laughed. His big arms came up blackened and burned like iron, and he slapped his hands together and stood with his legs apart. "Now we need music," he said. "And children. By God, we need children!"

Everyone was quiet then, and to the right of the crowd, the people moved apart. Tinker was there, with the rest of David's kids, and he was all squeaky clean, the way he would be for church. Emily was there, smiling, and for a moment David saw only that smile and he answered it with a private look. Then he held his hand out, and Tinker came forward.

"Come look," David said. "Come look and ride."

Of course Tinker had been there before, helped to build it, but it was different now. David took Tinker and the other kids into his arms, a great sweep of burned-black arms, and he gave them a personal tour of what he had done.

"Come and see what the steel did," he said, putting Tinker on the Ferris wheel. "See what it did for you." He kicked the motor over. It started, and Tinker went up and over with a smile that spread all across his face.

"Everybody come," David said then, turning. "Everybody come now. It's for everybody."

Everyone moved at once. Somebody brought an accordian, and somebody else brought a fiddle. Children appeared from everywhere. Booths were filled with games and food, and we fired up the engines on the rides. The sounds of the motors mixed with the music and the squeals of the kids as they rode up and around and down, and David just walked around and through it. I've never seen a man so happy. It was a happy that matched the sad he had been that night at the table staring down at his hands, a happy that lifted him right off the ground.

When night came, nothing turned down or stopped, but I was beyond tired into numb, cleaned-out numb.

I walked with Jenny once more through what we had made, through the noise and movement and joy, and I saw David eating a big rolled-up lefse full of jelly.

"Jenny," I said, "I don't know how I could have been what I was back in the city. I stand here now, and I don't know how I could have done those things. I was tearing things down, and all the time there were people like David who made these things, and I was just ripping them apart."

I wanted to say more, but I couldn't because it wouldn't come out right. Jenny knew what I meant, and she touched my cheek, and we walked away from the circus and sat for a long time on the short grass. I told her about what I wanted to be and do, and the circus went on and on.

About the Author

<<<<<<<<<<<<<<<<<<<<<<<<<<<<<<<<<<<<<<<<<<<<<<<<<<<<

A native of the Minnesota he writes about so vividly, GARY PAULSEN records his past occupations as "electronics engineer, soldier, actor, director, carpenter, dynamite handler, teacher, lecturer, farmer, political writer, adman, heavy-equipment operator, folk singer, truck driver." But at heart he is surely a writer, with a long list of books to his credit, including *The Spitball Gang*, *Winterkill*, *The Foxman*, *Tiltawhirl John*, and *The Night the White Deer Died*.

Mr. Paulsen is married and has a son. He has recently taken a dogsled team of huskies across Alaska.

Five powerful novels from Gary Paulsen, a two-time Newbery Honor winner:

_____ 0-14-032241-8 DANCING CARL   **$3.99**
Carl looked like a bum, but his power and his dancing were real magic.

_____ 0-14-032235-3 DOGSONG   **$4.50**
Inspired by an Eskimo shaman, Russel Suskitt and his dog team escape modern life to find their "true" song.
A Newbery Honor Book

_____ 0-14-032724-X HATCHET   **$3.99**
A boy survives a plane crash but has only the clothes he is wearing and a hatchet with which to keep himself alive.
A Newbery Honor Book

_____ 0-14-032239-6 SENTRIES   **$4.99**
As four teenagers' lives unfold in different parts of the country, their common hope leads them on converging paths.

_____ 0-14-032240-X TRACKER   **$3.99**
John must track the doe not to kill it, but to find through the skill the way to hold on to his dying grandfather's life.
